MISS KANE'S CHRISTMAS

A CHRISTMAS CENTRAL ROMANTIC COMEDY

CAROLINE MICKELSON

BON ACCORD PRESS

"I cannot believe you've banished me from the North Pole." Carol Claus glanced across the sleigh at her father. "What have I done?"

"Don't be so melodramatic, my dear." Santa smiled at his daughter. He hopped down from the driver's seat and motioned for Carol to join him. When she did, he put his arm around her shoulders and gave her an affectionate hug. He gestured across the moonlit neighborhood of Indian Village. "This is a beautiful place for you to spend your first Christmas away from home."

Carol looked down on the snow covered street. Each two story home in the cul-de-sac was bedecked with strings of colored lights, nativity scenes, plastic gift wrapped lawn ornaments, and pine wreaths on the front doors. The seventh home just under their feet was the exception to the neighborhood's festive spirit. A white clapboard colonial with black shutters, it gave no indication that its owners knew Christmas was only three days away.

She fixed a pleading expression on her father but, while his blue eyes sparkled with his love for her, he showed no sign of going back on his decision that she spend her first Christmas with a family of his choosing. It was a Claus family tradition, and Carol, as the youngest child, was over-due for her turn. Still, she made one last ditch effort to change his mind. "You've said yourself that no one excels at elf management like I do."

"True, I said it and I meant it. But your absence will give your brother Nicholas a chance to work more closely with the elves. Besides, you deserve some fun this year. You work too hard."

"I love every moment of it." Carol tucked a strand of her dark hair behind her ear. She shared her father's blue eyes and his love of Christmas. "I'll miss you, Daddy."

"I'll miss you too, my girl. I know this won't be easy, Carol, but it's necessary." He dug into the pocket of his red down jacket and pulled out a sheet of folded paper. "Read this."

She reached out for the paper. "What is it?"

"Just read it. It's the reason you're here."

Carol unfolded the slightly crumpled sheet of lined paper and instantly recognized that it had been written by a child. Fortunately the moon was bright enough to allow her to easily read the words that had been neatly printed in crayon.

. . .

DEAR SANTA,

MY DADDY DOESN'T KNOW I'm writing to you. He would say I can't write a letter to someone who doesn't even exist but I know you are real. My Mom told me so before she died. My little brother Patrick doesn't remember her saying that but that's only because she was gone before he was even in preschool. I'm not writing to ask for anything for Patrick or me. But Santa, can you please bring my Daddy some happiness? I know the elves can't wrap it, and it's nothing you can bring down the chimney but he needs help. I don't know who else to ask. I know you'll think of something Santa.

from Hillary (age 8)

P.S. Patrick likes to play with cars and my favorite color is pink

CAROL FINISHED READING THE LETTER, refolded it and handed it back to her father. "I take it we're at Hillary and Patrick's house?"

Santa nodded. "And not a moment too soon, my dear. There are three very sad people living here. I can't bear for them to suffer through one more miserable holiday."

"You're so kind hearted, Daddy." Carol knew she was beat. She couldn't say no to her father, not when little Hillary was counting on Santa Claus, and Santa Claus was counting on her. "There's more to it than you're telling me, isn't there?"

Her father nodded. "Quite a bit more."

"Tell me what's going on then. I'd rather know going in what I'm up against." Carol stomped her feet to keep some feeling in them. "Is this about the children's mother?"

"No. The children were too young to know that their mother had all but left their father just before she was diagnosed with cancer. She'd already rented a townhome and had packed up most of her things but then she found out she was ill. Her husband insisted she move into the guest room to recover."

"Except that she didn't," Carol guessed. "Recover, I mean."

Santa nodded.

"She was going to leave the children with their father?" she asked for clarification. "There was no custody fight?"

"No. She made it clear she was not willing to be a full-time parent."

"So this Ben Hanson is broken hearted over his wife's plan to leave him and her death, and his grief is spilling over onto the children?"

"No, that's not it. Of course, there's been some

sadness to work through but the family seems to be doing remarkably well in most ways."

"Where do I fit in? I don't understand what you want me to do, Daddy."

"Ben Hanson has issues with Christmas."

"Define issues."

Santa blew out a long sigh, his breath quickly turning into a puff of smokey air. "He's a sports writer by trade but he's working on a book that has me worried." He shook his head wearily. "He's writing it with such conviction that I'm afraid it's going to take hold in more than a few parents' minds."

Carol eyed her father thoughtfully. She'd never seen him upset by a single cynic before. "What's the title of his book?"

"Beyond Bah Humbug: Why Lying to Your Child about Santa is a Bad Idea."

"Oh," Carol said, suddenly understanding her father's concern. "Not good."

"Precisely."

At least it was clear what she was doing here now. "You want me to get his manuscript and destroy it, is that my mission?"

Santa Claus frowned. "Of course not, we're not going to save Christmas by resorting to petty theft and destruction of another person's property. Besides, he's bound to have it saved to an external hard drive."

"Then what do you want me to do?"

"I want you to be yourself." Santa's face lit up. "Just be yourself, Carol. You've always held the true

Christmas spirit in your heart, now go and share that joy with the Hanson family. You see, I think we should not only help Mr. Hanson learn to love Christmas, I think we should turn him into one of our ambassadors. Brilliant idea, if I do say so myself."

Brilliant wasn't the word Carol would have used. Her father, every jolly ounce of him, was an eternal optimist. Christmas ambassadors were adults who believed in the story of Santa and the magic of Christmas. According to her father, these ambassadors were essential to keeping the tradition of Santa Claus alive.

Carol quickly did the mental math. Her father wanted her to take this Ben Hanson from humbug to ho ho ho in just a few days?

"The children of the world are counting on us, Carol. We cannot let them down."

Carol didn't hold out much hope for her success but she knew she had to try. Her father was counting on her and she wouldn't, couldn't, let him down. Every child mattered to Santa. That was one of the things she loved most about her father. "I'll miss you."

"I'll miss you too, my girl." Santa held out his arms and Carol gave him a farewell hug before he hopped back into the sleigh. He picked up the reins. "Call me any time you need me."

Carol nodded but she knew she wouldn't do so unless it was an emergency. The next few days were a whirlwind of non-stop activity at the North Pole. She didn't doubt that her father, or her mother and brother for that matter, would be there for her. But she needed to handle this on her own. Just how, she had no clue.

"Any special instructions?" she asked hopefully.

Santa thought for a moment. "Just one thought, try not to absorb the Hanson's sadness. Let them soak up your joy instead. Now, I must dash." He blew her a kiss. "Merry Christmas, my girl."

"Wait, Dad," Carol called just as he snapped the reins. "Can you at least get me off the roof?"

"Sorry, dear." Santa quickly tapped his finger to his nose and Carol was transported to the Hanson's front door. She looked up into the clear night sky and waved a forlorn goodbye to the rapidly disappearing sleigh. Merry Christmas indeed.

She lifted her suitcase and rang the front doorbell.

THE CHIMING of the front door bell awoke Ben Hanson from a fitful sleep. He lay in bed wondering if he'd imagined the sound. No, there it was again. He threw back the covers, grabbed his worn terry robe and slipped into it. He stuffed his feet into slippers that were just as worn and shuffled over to the window. He peered down onto the moonlit yard but couldn't see a car out front. He did hear someone knocking on the door.

Ben ran a hand through his tousled hair and grabbed his wire rimmed glasses from the bed side table. He checked in on his son and daughter but they

7

were sleeping. He ran lightly down the stairs and flicked on the porch light. Keeping the chain in place, he opened the door just wide enough that he could peek out.

A young woman in a cherry red wool coat stood on the doorstep. Although she wore a knit beret it didn't cover either her dark brown bobbed hair or shadow her face. A face that was looking quite alert and enthusiastic considering it was two o'clock in the morning.

"Can I help you?" he asked.

"Hello, Mr. Hanson." The stranger smiled.

Ben's mind raced to place the woman's face. He wasn't overly friendly with the neighbors but he was fairly sure this young woman wasn't a neighbor. He'd remember if he'd seen her before. Yet she knew him. Or at least his name, which put him at a disadvantage.

"I'm sorry, I don't know you."

"I'm Carol Kane." She looked at him expectantly.

"What can I do for you Miss Kane?" As innocent as she looked, Ben kept his hand on the door knob, ready to slam it shut should she tell him she was there to recruit him for her cult."I'm the new au pair." She smiled. "May I come in?"

Au pair? This wasn't right. "You aren't supposed to be here until January," he said.

"I'm here now." Another smile. "May I come in?"

Ben hesitated. What on earth was she doing here in the middle of the night? At least a week early?

"Do you have any documentation? Proof of who you are?"

His question didn't appear to faze her. In fact, she seemed very prepared as she reached into her purse and pulled out a sheaf of papers. She slipped them through the door crack.

"Here you are, Mr. Hanson. My letter from the agency, my resume and my passport."

Ben quickly flipped through the papers. Carol Kane, age twenty-four, five feet five inches tall. He opened the passport and immediately recognized the cheery face in the photo as the same young woman who now stood on his doorstep. He handed the papers back to her through the barely opened door.

"Thank you, Mr. Hanson. May I come in?" she asked again.

"Yes, of course, sorry." Ben undid the chain and opened the door. He stepped back as Carol entered the hallway. She had one small, round, red vintage Samsonite suitcase with her. Her wool coat, her suitcase and handbag were vintage as well. But there was nothing shabby about Carol Kane. Quite the opposite, she was young, pert, cheery and, he had no doubt, quite enthusiastic in everything she did.

He started to wonder if he hadn't just made a huge mistake.

"I apologize for my late arrival," Carol said. "Transportation from where I come from isn't quite as reliable as you'd imagine."

Ben shook his head. "You're not late, Miss Kane. I wasn't expecting you until early January."

"I thought I'd come in time for the holidays."

Ben stared at her. Huge mistake it was. Granted she was the first au pair he'd ever hired, and heaven knew he needed help with the kids, but he hadn't expected a hired babysitter to show up looking as if she were a long lost relative finally home for the holidays.

"We don't really celebrate the holidays," he managed to say.

Carol looked around the hallway and over his shoulder into the living room. "I can see that. Is it a religious issue?"

"No. I just don't like Christmas." He pushed his glasses up higher on the bridge of his nose.

"Hard to imagine," Carol said. "I love Christmas. It's a joyous time of the year. I'm sure we can manage to celebrate-"

Ben held up his hand. "Stop right there, Miss Kane. We won't be having any part of Christmas this year."

"Why not?" Her expression wasn't judgmental but more curious than anything. "Does it make you sad?"

Her words set off alarm bells in Ben's mind. This wasn't going to work. She needed to go. "Miss Kane, I'm afraid there's been a huge misunderstanding. I'm not going to be needing help with my children after all. Let me call a taxi for you. There's a hotel not far from here."

He turned to the hall table and picked up the address book. He flipped through it, trying to remember if he'd put the number under C for cab or T for taxi.

He looked up in surprise when she laid her hand on his sleeve.

"Surely you don't mean to send me out to a strange hotel in the middle of the night?" Carol asked. "Wouldn't it be possible for you to put me up for the night at least?"

Ben hesitated, torn between the desire to do the right thing and the desire to reclaim his quiet, predictable, orderly household. What had he been thinking, hiring a stranger to live in his house?

"I would be perfectly content to sit in the kitchen if you don't have a room ready," she said. "Please."

Ben felt like a heel. "I'm sorry, Miss Kane. Of course you can stay the night. The guest room is right down the hall." He picked up her suitcase, surprised at how light it was. "Follow me."

He led Carol down the hall, dropped her case in the guest room and then showed her where the bathroom was. "Well, I guess I'll see you in the morning." He stood in the doorway uncertainly. "I am sorry about the change in plans."

Carol's smile was bright. "Don't worry, Mr. Hanson. I'm sure things will work out just as they're meant to."

CHAPTER 2

As she did every day, Carol awoke the next morning ready to greet the world with a million watt smile. She loved the early mornings at the North Pole, especially the way the sun shone on the ice as if it were anointing the landscape with a golden light.

Carol drew back the curtains in the guest bedroom, then the living room, and finally the kitchen before she made a cursory inspection of the Hanson's home. Neat and orderly, tidy to a fault actually, their home was nonetheless depressing. There was not one sign of Christmas anywhere. No tree, no manger, no stockings hung with care. Nothing. Nada. Zippo. Carol shook her head. This was no way to live.

She'd arrived just in time.

First things first. She switched on the tiny built-in radio under the microwave and scanned until she found an all holiday music channel. As an instrumental

12

version of Sleigh Bells played she stood and surveyed the kitchen. No one else was yet awake but she was hungry. She bit her lip. Perhaps it would be overstepping to start cooking when poor Ben Hanson still didn't realize he was going to allow her to stay. No, she'd best wait until he caught up with the situation.

Ignoring her stomach's loud calls for her usual morning meal of Christmas cookies and a peppermint laced latte, she helped herself to a piece of paper and pen from beside the telephone. She'd start on the shopping list.

Cookie cutters, ingredients for the dough, and sprinkles received top billing. Coffee, mint tea and eggnog came in a close second. Candy canes were a must, and her personal favorites, red and green M & M's, rounded out the list of immediate needs.

On to a decorations list. The children would know best what color lights to buy for decorating the outside of the house. She'd leave that choice to them, but she couldn't help but think that as the neighbors seemed to favor colored lights, it would be nice if the children chose white icicle ones. Of course they needed some Christmas music. She added candles to the list. She didn't think it was proper to live in a house without an evergreen, cinnamon, or mint scent.

Decisions about the tree were a little trickier. Carol tapped the tip of her pen against the table. Tree decorations were so personal, here she was reluctant to overstep.

"Hello," a voice called out.

Carol whirled around in her chair. A sleepy little boy stood in the doorway, holding tight to a raggedy blanket. Carol smiled. "Well, hello. You must be Patrick."

The little boy nodded. "Who are you?"

"My name is Carol," she told him.

"What are you doing here?" he asked.

Carol smiled. In looks and demeanor the child reminded her of his father. In fact, Patrick looked like a miniature Ben Hanson. He had the same light brown hair, the same intense gaze, and an aura of sweet bewilderment that pulled at her heart.

"I've come to help take care of you and your sister. I met your father when I arrived last night but you and Hillary were already asleep."

Patrick entered the kitchen and sat at the table across from Carol, all the while keeping a tight grip on his blanket. She was relieved to see he didn't seem frightened by her presence, merely curious.

"Shall I help you find some breakfast?" Carol asked. Her actual face to face experience with children was quite limited she realized. Because so much of her family's life revolved around bringing joy to children at the holiday time she felt like she knew a lot about children. But now, as she sat across from Patrick, she realized she wasn't quite as prepared for this experience as she'd thought. "Are you hungry?"

Patrick shook his head. "No."

"Do you have school today?" Carol asked.

Patrick shook his head again. "We're on break."

"Oh, that's quite nice, isn't it?" Carol smiled again, wishing that the little boy would do the same. "What sort of fun do you and Hillary have planned for your days off?"

"We don't have fun here."

Carol tried not to stare. But really, this was the last response she'd expected to hear. "How old are you Patrick?"

"Six," he said. "I'm in kindergarten."

"Then isn't having fun technically your job?" Carol asked.

Patrick was saved from having to answer by the arrival of his sister. Hillary shared her brother's resemblance to their father. But unlike her brother, who was attired in his pajamas still, Hillary was fully dressed in a red argyle sweater worn with brown corduroy pants. Her outfit was completed by a pink tulle skirt worn over her pants.

"Good morning, Hillary. I'm Carol." She smiled, and was relieved when Hillary smiled back. "I'm here to help take care of you."

Hillary stuck out her hand and shook Carol's. "It's nice to meet you. What is your last name?"

"Kane," she supplied. "My full name is Carol Candy Kane but no one calls me that. I think it would sound awfully silly, don't you?"

Both children nodded and giggled. Candy Kane had been Santa's idea of a little joke when she'd been born. But it came in handy now as going by Carol Claus was just a little too obvious.

"Now, shall we get down to some serious business?" Carol asked.

Wide eyed, the children nodded.

"Wonderful. Let's find a deck of cards."

"Good morning, Miss Kane." Ben stopped in the entrance way to the kitchen, caught off guard by his children's laughter. It wasn't a sound he often heard, especially in the mornings. He looked from his son to his daughter. "What's so funny?"

They smiled at him but it was Carol who spoke next, and it didn't escape his notice that she neatly sidestepped his question.

"Good morning, Mr. Hanson. The children and I were just getting acquainted."

Ben looked at the children in turn. They seemed remarkably composed considering they'd awoken to find a stranger in the kitchen. But his children were usually composed, which was one of his worries. He frowned.

"Ah, I take it you must be a first-thing-in-the-morning coffee drinker," Carol said. "If you could point me in the direction of the right cupboard I can make a quick pot."

He glanced at his watch. "No time. We need to get going if we're to drop you off at the airport in time."

"In time for what?" Carol asked. "I don't have a flight scheduled."

Ben stared at her. Her composure was remarkable. She seemed perfectly at ease sitting in his kitchen, playing cards with his children as if she were an old family friend. The fact he was in an obvious hurry to be rid of her didn't appear to faze her at all.

He reached into his pocket and pulled out his cell phone. "That's easily fixed, tell me what city you need to end up in and I'll book a flight." He flicked his finger across the screen looking for an airline schedule. "I'm sure we can find you something."

"Even with holiday travel being as busy as it is?"

He fixed yet another curious glance on Carol. She was young as far as nannies went, but certainly she was old enough to know when she wasn't wanted? In every other way she appeared to be socially appropriate. He must have been crazy to think that the solution to his child care problems was inviting a stranger into his home. He glanced between Hillary and Patrick. No, not crazy. Just desperate.

"Which airport did you say would work best for you?" he asked again.

"I didn't." Carol stood and gathered up the deck of cards and handed them to his daughter. "Hillary, dear, why don't you and Patrick go set the game up in the living room. I'll be right there. And remember, six cards for each of us."

Ben moved aside as the children obediently left the kitchen. He couldn't deny that the children looked perfectly at ease with Carol. He, however, was quickly becoming disquieted by the ease with which she was fitting into his household.

"Mr. Hanson, first let me say that I completely understand your qualms about leaving the children with someone you don't know well, but please do remember that you reviewed my resume, references and clearances yourself. You must have been satisfied enough to engage me to watch the children. Might I know why you've changed your mind?"

He hesitated, feeling slightly on the defensive. "I just feel that, well, it seems that I underestimated how great the change would be if someone actually moved in here."

"Ah, you're nervous then." Carol nodded her head as if the entire situation suddenly made sense. "I'm sure that after a few days we'll have settled into a routine. When you're home with the children I will be in my room or I'll arrange to be out so that you don't feel uncomfortable."

Ben put a finger under his shirt collar and wiggled it around for some more breathing space. Uncomfortable was the perfect word for the idea of having this lovely, composed young woman in his home.

"Well, you see, the thing is that my work is quite demanding this time of year so I won't actually be home very much-"

"All the more reason you need me here then," Carol said. "Unless you have a backup plan? Someone who can work days, nights, and weekends presumably? Someone who can devote themselves to Hillary and

Patrick so they can enjoy their holiday school break as much as possible?'

The young woman should be a lawyer, not a nanny, he thought. With the ability to pounce on his words and turn them around, she'd be in high demand in courtrooms across America.

"Why don't you let me stay for the day and we can discuss it this evening when you're home from work?" Carol suggested. "It would give you all day to make other arrangements and it would give me time to make some plans."

Ben found himself nodding, if only in relief that he could get to the office where he always thought more clearly than he did at home. It was a safe zone where he didn't think about the mess he was making of trying to raise the children himself. But he could do this. He could find a way out of this, find a child care solution that would be adequate. "Okay, then, one day. And I do apologize for the inconvenience and change of plans."

"Not to worry," Carol said. "I understand perfectly."

He believed her. She spoke with a calm, confident manner that left him with no doubt she handled children skillfully, adults too for that matter.

He gathered his coat and brief case from the hall closet. Feeling slightly guilty that he was so relieved to be leaving the house, he kissed each of his children on the forehead and then patted them on the top of the head. He opened his mouth to remind Hillary that she shouldn't be wearing a tutu over her clothes but he stopped himself. He could sort that out later.

With a last wave, he shut the front door behind him. He inhaled the cold, fresh morning air. This whole mess would all work itself out, he didn't have to worry. By this time tomorrow he'd have new child care plans in place. Ones that didn't involve a beautiful young woman living in his home.

He stepped off the first step, right onto an icy second step. His feet flew out from under him. He reached out for the wrought iron railing but missed and landed on his side. A sharp pain shot through his entire body right before he blacked out.

CHAPTER 3

"A mild concussion and a sprained shoulder is all that ails your friend." The emergency room physician shut her laptop and smiled reassuringly at Carol and the children. She handed a few slips of paper to Carol. "I recommend that Mr. Hanson take the remainder of the week off and rest at home with very limited activity. There are care instructions in your discharge papers, and you're welcome to call the triage number if anything comes up."

"Thank you, Doctor." Carol smiled her thanks before bundling Hillary and Patrick through the double swinging doors that led back into the waiting room. "See, you heard for yourselves straight from the doctor's mouth that your father is going to be just fine," she assured them.

"Can we go home now?" Patrick asked as he shrugged into his jacket. "I'm tired."

Carol bent down to help him zip it up. Made with down feathers, it was toasty warm but it made Patrick's arms stick straight out. His puffer jacket was black and his knit cap was white. He looked like a penguin. She ignored a stab of homesickness that shot through her.

"Yes, we can go now. We just need to wait for your-" she broke off as a nurse brought Ben out in a wheelchair. His arm was in a sling and his face resembled a storm cloud. "There he is." She waved cheerily, refusing to let her smile slip. Christmas was only days away and she had too much to do to get ready for it to waste time being unhappy.

"I'll just go bring the car around," she said immediately after the nurse departed. She asked the children to wait with their father and then headed for the parking lot. A few moments later she swung the Hanson's Toyota Highlander in front of the urgent care doors and jumped out to help Ben into the front seat.

"Easy does it," she said as she slipped her hand under his good arm. "Hillary and Patrick, you two hop into your seats and buckle yourselves in."

Ben took a few steps but then stopped abruptly. "What happened to my car?"

Carol managed not to bump into him, but just barely. "What are you talking about?" she asked, although she already knew what had him staring at the SUV in horror.

"Are those antlers on the front of my car?" His voice sounded an octave higher than she'd heard it before.

But perhaps that was just the pain meds kicking in. "Is that a red ball strapped to the grill?"

"Of course it's not a red ball," Carol said. "It's Rudolph's nose."

"Rudolph's what?" he practically shouted. He stared down at her. "When did you have the time to-"

His question was interrupted by the sound of an incoming ambulance siren. Knowing the car needed to be moved, he allowed Carol to help him into the seat but he continued to frown as she drove out of the hospital lot and turned onto the main road.

"How about some Christmas music?" she asked. Considering it a rhetorical question, she reached over and switched on the radio. She fiddled with the knob until she heard Elvis's Blue Christmas. Perfect. She loved Elvis. And it was a fitting song because it would be a blue Christmas if she couldn't find a way to get Ben Hanson to stop frowning at every mention of anything holiday related. She turned the music up just loud enough to discourage him from further conversation, specifically from asking questions about the packages overflowing in the third row seat.

She shot him a sideways glance. He looked miserable. Could some of it be due to his physical pain? Perhaps. But before he'd slipped and fallen that morning, he'd seemed just as awkward. She glanced in the rear view mirror. The children's intense little faces seemed uncertain. Despite spending a limited amount of time with the Hanson family, Carol would consider it a safe bet that Ben loved his children and they him.

And at their ages, and without their mother, they certainly needed him.

Didn't children always need their fathers? Even at her age she still delighted in spending time with her father, and when upset or confused she sought Santa's council. And when she and her brother Nicholas had been Hillary and Patrick's age they'd loved nothing more than going for a ride in Santa's sleigh. On dark nights just like this one they'd gone for long rides, practice runs Santa had called them, and they'd taken such delight in looking at Christmas lights and chatting with their father.

An uneasy sensation stirred within her. This situation wasn't right. Not at all.

And then Carol heard her father's voice, her memory playing one of his favorite expressions as if it were a tape recording, "If it's wrong, you just have to make it right."

As she drove past a house with a huge inflatable Santa in the front yard, Carol smiled. She now knew just what her father wanted her to do. It was time for some good old-fashioned Christmas magic and she knew just who to call in as reinforcements.

BEN SANK INTO HIS RECLINER, grateful to be off of his feet and even more grateful to be home. Rest, the doctor had said. As if. She hadn't a clue that his house was being invaded by the Christmas spirit. And instead of the joyous feeling the season was supposed to invoke, he felt as if he were falling head first into a bottomless pit of sadness, loneliness and despair. And it was all Carol's fault.

He watched as she and the children brought in yet another armload of packages from the car. He opened his mouth to object but closed it again. Whatever was in those Target bags wasn't the problem. It was her. Carol. She was the problem. And if he could get rid of her then everything else could be taken care of with one simple call to Goodwill.

Pain shot through his arm as he tried to rise. Damn. Of all of the fool times to fall and hurt himself this had to be the worst. Twelve years he'd lived in the house, hundreds of times he'd used the front steps but today was the first time he had slipped on the ice. As much as he hated to admit it, it did change everything. How could he send Carol away without other child care lined up? He would need help now more than ever, but that didn't have to mean it had to be Carol. Surely there were agencies for this sort of thing?

"Hillary," he called out. No answer. "Patrick?" he tried again.

"Yes, Dad?" his son stuck his head in the living room.

"Bring me the phone please."

Patrick shook his head. "I can't, Miss Kane's using it."

"I need my cell phone then. I think it's on the kitchen counter, or maybe the hall table." He started to get up. "It could also be in my jacket pocket. Let me look."

"Sit down. I can find it." Patrick left but returned not a second later. "Don't worry, Dad. If I can't find it, Miss Kane will know just where it is."

Don't worry? He couldn't do anything but.

He smiled gratefully when his son placed the phone in his outstretched hand but waited until Patrick was gone before sliding up the top to expose the keyboard. Texting with one hand proved to be more difficult than he thought so instead he punched in his sister's phone number and waited for her to pick up.

"Ben?" He heard his sister's sleepy voice greet him. "What time is it?"

He'd forgotten about the time difference. "Sorry, Cecily. Did I disturb you?"

"It's the middle of the night here, so yes you did but it's okay." And then he heard her tone change to one of panic. "Are Hillary and Patrick okay? What's happened?"

"They're fine, just fine. They miss you though."

A curious silence hung between them. Now that he had his sister on the line he felt foolish. Asking, or even hinting, that he needed her help, was unfair. She'd done so much, given so much, heck, she'd given up her life after Tami died to devote herself to the children. This was the first time in three years that she'd left them. And he was a heel to even think of asking her to cancel her trip and come home.

"I miss them too. Now, what's the matter? Is this about your shoulder?" Cecily asked.

Ben nearly dropped the phone. "How did you know?"

"Carol told me."

Ben was at a loss for words. Polite words anyway. His irritation was fast outweighing the pain in his shoulder.

"You talked to her?"

"Yep. She was kind enough to call and tell me about your fall. I think it was incredibly thoughtful of her, don't you?" When he didn't answer, his sister continued, "I have to confess that I've felt horribly guilty about leaving you and the children at Christmas time. But talking to Carol made me feel so much better about it all."

"I bet it did," was all Ben could manage to say.

"It was the best Christmas gift I could have hoped to receive. She sounds delightful, and Patrick and Hillary sound happy too. We couldn't have gotten any luckier, Ben. Now, tell me again why you called? Is something wrong?"

Something? Try everything. But Ben couldn't bring himself to drag his sister into his misgivings. He took a deep breath. "I knew your flight to London left in the morning and I just wanted to wish you well."

They chatted for a few more moments before he hung up. He leaned his head back and closed his eyes. He was suddenly glad he hadn't disrupted his sister's plans. Cecily sounded happy and she deserved that. He trusted her judgment implicitly, especially when it came to the children.

Get it together, Ben, he told himself. Three weeks. He could keep things together for three weeks until Cecily was home and then together they could look for a new nanny. He could make the best of this. He opened his eyes and started to get up but then he froze. He shook his head and rubbed his eyes.

There was an elf in the hallway. He blinked several times. An elf?

CHAPTER 4

C arol grabbed ahold of Tinsel's shoulder and pulled him back into the kitchen by the scruff of his green felt collar. "Get in here," she hissed. "Quick, before anyone sees you."

"What?" Tinsel objected. "Why are you acting like this? We're here to help you."

"Well it won't help me if you're seen," Carol shot back. She threw up her hands. "Look, Tinsel, please go back out to the garage and wait with Jolly until everyone has gone to bed."

"Rapz is here with us too," Tinsel said, his voice suddenly a stage whisper.

"What?" Carol sounded frantic and she knew it, but she couldn't help it. The day had been long. She'd never lived in such a Christmas hostile environment. Acting casual about the holidays was proving to be exhausting. She closed her eyes for a second. Focus, Carol, she instructed herself. Breathe deeply. She was a seasoned professional who managed over twelve hundred elves, often under very hectic circumstances. She could handle this. "Rapz is a loose cannon. Why couldn't he have just stayed in the wrapping department?"

"Nicholas said-"

"Nicholas?" Carol shook her head. So this was her brother's doing, his idea of a joke. She should have known her father wouldn't send a wrapper elf. Like all of Santa's helpers, Rapz's heart was in the right place. But he paid more attention to wearing just the right sun glasses and gold chains than he did to all the little details that were necessary to make Christmas magical. "Never mind what my brother said. I just need you three to stay out of sight until I can get everyone to sleep and the house is quiet."

Tinsel winked, clearly finding the situation amusing. "Can do."

"Miss Kane?" Ben's voice called from the living room. "What's going on in there?"

She cringed. Oh, holy holiday, had he heard Tinsel?

"I'll be right there, Mr. Hanson," she answered. She shooed Tinsel in the direction of the garage. "Just stay out of sight." She turned back to the elf. "Go on. I'll get them all upstairs and then I'll come get you."

As soon as Tinsel slipped into the garage, Carol headed toward the living room but she took only a few steps before she bumped straight into Ben Hanson.

"Owww." Ben staggered backward and held up his

good hand to keep Carol from coming any closer. "Who's in the kitchen with you?"

"No one." Carol reached out but he backed away.

"I heard voices." Ben's voice held an accusatory tone.

"Voices?" Carol shook her head. "The medicine must be playing tricks on you." She tried to maneuver him back into the living room but he wouldn't budge. "Do you want me to call the doctor?"

"No, I don't want you to call the doctor." He drew his brows together in an expression that was equal parts confusion and annoyance.

Ben's frown, Carol decided, was rather attractive. She smiled. She couldn't help herself.

"And just what is so funny?" Ben demanded.

"I always smile during the holidays," Carol said. "Now, we really need to get you up to bed." She gently turned him toward the staircase. "Let's say goodnight to the children and then get you between the sheets."

First he thought he saw an elf and now he was imagining that the new nanny was propositioning him. What exactly was in those painkillers?

He allowed Carol to guide him up the stairs but he stopped outside of his bedroom door. "Goodnight, then, Miss Kane." He looked down into her upturned face with its expectant blue eyes. She appeared to be

31

waiting for him to say something. "Umm...thank you. For your help today, I mean."

"You're welcome." Carol reached right around him and turned the door handle. His bedroom door swung open. "In bed, Mr. Hanson. I'll bring the children to say goodnight in just a moment."

Ben took a step backward into his room. He hated to appear ungrateful but with all the time they'd spend in urgent care they still hadn't had the chance to discuss her departure. And depart she must. Every time he looked into Carol's eyes he felt like he was walking into a trap. A dangerous trap. He cleared his throat. "Miss Kane, there's something I need-"

A resounding crash sounded from downstairs. "What the devil?" Ben took a step forward but Carol blocked the doorway.

"Didn't you hear that?" he demanded.

"Hear what?"

"That loud crashing sound?"

Carol raised her eyebrows. "It was probably just a box that fell over. I'll pop down and check if you like. I'm sure it's nothing though."

If it was nothing, Ben wondered, then why did he see a tiny flicker of something in her eyes? Surprise? Concern? And why did she keep glancing over her shoulder? "What's going on?" he demanded.

Carol smiled her maddeningly reassuring smile. "Why don't we get you ready for bed and I'll nip downstairs to see what happened?"

Ben stared at her incredulously. He wasn't one of

her charges. He opened his mouth but clamped it shut just as quickly. He was tired. And the sooner the day was over the sooner he could send Miss Carol Kane on her way. It was easy to see how naturally good she was with the children, and she was an attractive young woman, he'd give her that. But, if the last twenty-four hours were any indication, he sensed that chaos followed this woman around. Closely.

"I don't need any help," he said. Yet she still stood there, watching him, her uncertainty palpable.

He shifted uncomfortably under her thoughtful gaze.

"Of course you do," Carol finally said. She crossed the room and reached for his shirt buttons before he realized what she was doing.

"Miss Kane, if you don't mind." He tried to pull back but her grip on his shirt was too tight. He looked down. She was fumbling with his buttons. "Now wait just a moment, I assure you I am fully capable-"

"Nonsense," she interrupted him. She undid the buttons on his shirt. "I'll get you into bed, I'll see to the children, and then I'll straighten up downstairs. I've just the few decorations to put up."

He trembled as Carol's fingers brushed against his skin. Of all the fantasies he'd ever had, being alone in his bedroom with a nanny dominatrix wasn't one of them. Good heavens, the door was open, his children were down the hall, and the young woman undressing him was as wholesome as, well, Christmas.

"I don't want the house overrun with tinsel and

Christmas paraphernalia," Ben protested as Carol slid his shirt off his good arm first and then, tenderly, over his injured arm. "Did you hear me?" He knew he sounded peevish, he could hear it. He hated being this out of control.

"Yes, I heard you but Christmas and paraphernalia are two words that don't belong in the same sentence. Now where do you keep your pajamas?"

"Top right dresser drawer." Self-conscious didn't begin to describe how he felt standing shirtless in the middle of his bedroom with a woman he barely knew. He watched her take out several pairs of pajamas and neatly set them aside. What was she looking for? "Any pair will do. The ones on the top are fine."

Carol turned to look at him over her shoulder. "Don't you have a Christmas pair?"

"A Christmas pair of what?"

"Never mind, we'll just add it to the list." She shook out a blue plaid flannel top. "Slip your arm in, easy does it." She deftly helped him ease his good arm into the other sleeve. "Now stand still so I can button this up."

"I can button it myself," he protested. "And I can get into the bottoms without any help."

Carol raised an eyebrow. "Really? That should be interesting to see."

Ben stared down at her. Her eyes were the most amazing shade of blue. Disconcertingly blue. He lifted his gaze to the ceiling.

"Okay, you can help me," he conceded. "Just with the top, I mean." He wanted to be alone so he could regain his equilibrium but there were limits, for heavens sake.

"Thank you, now stand still."

He wished she'd hurry with her ministrations because the effect she was having on him was unnerving. He waited impatiently while Carol buttoned his pajama top. She took his sling from the bed and set his arm in it so gently that he felt only a little pain.

"It's not quite right," she said. "Let me retie it."

"Just leave it," Ben grumbled, "It's fine."

Carol stood back, head cocked to the side, and studied his sling. "It's not fine. It's crooked and I can't seem to get it right." She reached her arms up around his neck. "Can you bend forward a little, Mr. Hanson? I can't reach quite reach the knot."

Just to get it over with, Ben did as he was told. He heard the shrill ring of the land line from the table in the hall. He almost asked Carol to answer it but stopped himself. There was no one he wanted to talk to. Not in the mood he was in.

"I've got it loose," Carol said. "Now just hold still while I re-tie the knot."

Hold still? Where was he going to go? He was all but hugging Carol. If he moved an inch to left his nose would be buried in her hair. Against his better judgment, he closed his eyes and inhaled. She smelled of roses with just a hint of pine, he thought.

"There you are, all set," Carol stood back and looked up at him. "Winter Rose."

"What?"

"My perfume, it's called Winter Rose."

He searched her face. She looked the picture of pure innocence.

"Your perfume? I don't know what you're talking about," he finally managed to say.

"Okay, let's just go with that then." She stepped back and surveyed the room. "Will you need another blanket, do you think?"

"I don't need help getting into bed." Ben started to cross his arms over his chest but winced when he tried to lift his arm. He frowned at Carol. "You're fussing and it's unnecessary and annoying."

"If you say so, Mr. Hanson."

Ben watched as she pulled back the covers on the left side of his bed. He wanted her out of his bedroom before he grew any more uncomfortable. The sight of her plumping his pillows was almost too much for him. "I sleep on the other side of the bed."

"Sorry." Carol went around to the right side and pulled back the covers, shook out his pillow and stood back. "I want you in bed now."

Ben opened his mouth to respond but froze when he heard his daughter's voice behind him.

"He's too busy to talk to you, Grandma."

Ben slowly turned. He'd forgotten that the phone rang only moments before. And now Hillary stood in the doorway, her ratty pink tutu over her red thermal pajamas, the cordless phone up against her ear. She smiled at him but ignored his outstretched hand.

"What's he doing?" Hillary cocked her head and looked first at Carol and then at him. "I'm not entirely sure but I think the new nanny is trying to get him into bed."

CHAPTER 5

"Daddy looked so mad last night," Hillary said between bites of her star shaped sugar cookie. "Are you certain that we're allowed to eat these for breakfast?"

Cookie half way to her mouth, Carol paused. "Why ever not?"

The children exchanged startled glances. It was Hillary who answered, "Because children aren't supposed to eat cookies for breakfast."

"Didn't you know that?" Patrick asked, his brow knit into a frown that was so much like his father's that it made her smile. Patrick eyed her thoughtfully. "Did your mother really let you eat cookies for breakfast?"

"Let us? She insisted." Carol dunked her gingerbread man into her milk and did her best to ignore the wave of homesickness that washed over her. "Now, tell me what you think of the decorations."

"I love them!" Hillary beamed. "When I came downstairs this morning I thought I was in the wrong house. I've never seen so much sparkle in my life. I love all of the red and green everywhere."

High praise from a child who wore a pink tutu all the time.

"What about you Patrick?" Carol asked. "What do you think of the decorations?"

"It's fun. Did you do it all yourself?" he asked.

Carol nodded. She ignored a pang of guilt for taking all of the credit. It wasn't as if she could tell the children that she'd had the help of three elves. Rapz had volunteered to bake and he'd happily beatboxed in the kitchen while whipping up trays of cookies, tins of Christmas fudge and a cherry strudel for each neighbor in the cul-de-sac. Meanwhile, Tinsel and Jolly had done a beautiful job stringing strands of garland and white lights through evergreen boughs.

They'd had the foresight to bring holiday themed place mats and napkins to liven up both the dining and kitchen tables, as well as candlesticks and ornaments to hang from the light fixtures. Carol had seen to setting out an entire ceramic winter village, complete with cotton ball snow drifts, on every available surface in the family room.

They'd worked into the early morning hours and she'd been grateful for the cheerful company. But when the stockings were hung and the cookies packed away in their tins, she had barely been able to stand watching her three good-natured helpers leave. Not wanting to be alone amidst so much cheer, she'd gone to bed, only to find an envelope on her pillow. She'd immediately recognized her father's handwriting and torn open the envelope.

MY DEAR CAROL,

YOUR MOTHER and I miss you! Your brother is finding it hard to fill your cheerful and capable shoes (he'd never admit it though!). I know you miss us too but take heart because your assistance there is a great gift to all the children who find joy in believing in the story of Santa. Joy is the greatest gift we can give any child, remember that. You're in my heart, dear daughter, always. See you in Maui on the 27th!

LOVE,
Daddy

"WHAT'S WRONG WITH MISS KANE?" Patrick's voice sounded as if it were coming through a snow storm.

"Maybe it's sugar shock," Hillary sounded worried.

Carol shook her head. "I'm fine. I was just daydreaming. Now what were we talking about?"

"Patrick asked if you did all of the decorating by yourself?" Hillary repeated patiently.

"Of course, I did," Carol said. "Who else would have helped me?"

Hillary shrugged. "We thought maybe Daddy woke up and came downstairs to help you."

"No, your father was asleep all evening." Carol had checked several times but he hadn't so much as rolled over, fortunately for her. The children had slept the night through as well. Maybe sleeping soundly was a Hanson family trait.

It was a shame that Ben wasn't as friendly, open minded, or fun as his children had turned out to be. She knew she should go upstairs to check on him and see if he needed any help but the look on his face last night when he'd ordered her out of his room hadn't suggested that he was in a particular hurry to see her again.

"Do you think Daddy is terribly angry still?" Hillary asked.

Carol shook her head. "Of, course not. I don't think he was angry at all. I think his arm just hurt and he was grumpy."

Both children nodded, satisfied with her answer.

"What are we going to do today?" Patrick asked.

Carol couldn't help but return their bright smiles. She'd never spent much time with children but she could see now that she'd missed out on some serious fun.

"First I suggest we get our coats and boots on and head outside to make a proper snowman. Then we need to plan how and where to put all the lights we bought yesterday. Are you two any good at climbing trees?"

"We're like monkeys," Patrick assured her.

"Wonderful, as long you're talking about the kind of monkeys that can string lights." She grinned when they giggled. Her father was right, the holiday really was all about children. Or should be. A sudden understanding of what her father wanted her to do dawned on her. Beyond Bah Humbug her left foot. Ben Hanson, however handsome and charming she knew he could be, however sensitive and intelligent he was, had no right to ruin Christmas for an untold number of children with a book full of outright lies.

Santa did exist. Of course, she couldn't use her lineage as proof but she'd figure something out.

"After we've got the lights up we can deliver some baked goods to your neighbors."

"Why?" Hillary asked. Patrick looked just as curious as his sister.

"Because it's Christmas time, because it's the neighborly thing to do. And," Carol paused, trying to decide just how much to tell the children about her plans. Oh, for the love of fir trees, if she couldn't trust two innocent children, she couldn't trust anyone. "I was thinking we could invite the neighbors over for a…gathering."

"A gathering?" Patrick asked.

"A party," Hillary told him before looking at Carol with wonder in her eyes. "You mean a Christmas party here at the house? With the neighbors?"

"Well, yes, of course we can invite the neighbors but we don't have to stop there. What about your father's work friends? We can invite everyone from his office too."

"But we don't know their names," Patrick objected.

"Does your father have an address book?"

"Couldn't we use his contact list from his tablet?"

"Tablet, of course," Carol hadn't thought of that. She'd wrapped plenty of them but didn't quite know how they worked. "Do you think you could figure out how to get the names?"

Hillary managed to stop just short of scoffing at her. "Yeah, I'm eight. Of course I can."

Carol nodded. "Good. Now I'm going to need lots of help to make this the best party ever. Are you sure you like the idea?"

Their ensuing squeals of delight assured her they did. She lifted a hand to request permission to speak. Once granted she asked them the question that had been weighing on her mind, choosing her words extra carefully. "The whole point of throwing this party is to help your father get into the holiday spirit. So, do you think he might enjoy the party a bit more if we included him in the planning or if it were a total surprise?"

Neither child needed much time to think.

"Let's surprise him," Hillary said, her eyes wide.

"Definitely," Patrick agreed, nodding solemnly.

Exactly the answer Carol wanted to hear.

43

BEN STOOD at the top of the staircase and surveyed the damage to his home. As best he could tell a yule bomb had exploded while he'd been asleep. And he knew just who had detonated it.

"Miss Kane," he called out as he made his way down the stairs. His shoulder ached but it was nothing compared to the throbbing in his head.

He found her in the foyer, she was busy bundling the children into their coats.

She turned to smile at him. "Good morning. I trust you slept well?" Without waiting for an answer she turned back to Hillary and helped her fasten her tutu over her snow pants.

He opened his mouth to point out the ridiculous-ness of wearing a tutu outdoors but stopped himself. He watched the children pull their mittens on. Their eyes were shining. Shining. He couldn't remember ever seeing them look so happy.

"Do you want to come outside with us, Daddy?" Hillary asked.

"After I have some coffee, honey, I will."

"Don't forget to eat your breakfast," Patrick piped up. "We had some delicious-"

But just what his son had for breakfast was to remain a mystery because Hillary's right hand clamped firmly over her brother's mouth. Ben had an idea that they'd sweet talked Carol into substituting the bran cereal he preferred they eat with frosted flakes or something equally unhealthy.

Carol stood. "We'll just be outside if you need

anything." She opened the front door. "There's a pot of tea on the stove and fresh coffee in the coffee maker. I wasn't sure which you preferred."

"Wait just a moment, Miss Kane. I need to speak with you."

"And I need to supervise the children outside." She shrugged. "But I'm sure we can fit in a talk sometime today."

Nice try. "No. Now is better." He turned to his children. "You two may play right in the front area outside the kitchen window. Miss Kane and I will both have an eye on you and we'll be out shortly."

They hastily agreed to his terms and scrambled out the door, doubtless wanting to get out before he changed his mind.

He nodded in the direction of the kitchen. "May I have a word?"

"Certainly, Mr. Hanson. I can see you have something on your mind."

He watched as Carol took down a mug from the cupboard. It amazed him how comfortable she appeared to be in his home and with his children. Was she like this everywhere she went?

"Coffee or tea?" she asked him.

"Coffee," he said, and then settled himself at the kitchen table. His shoulder ached but he'd had a surprisingly good night's sleep. Which wasn't such a good thing as it turned out. If he'd been tossing and turning last night maybe he'd have heard Carol creating havoc and could have put a stop to her decorating. At least it would have saved her the trouble of packing it all up today.

"What did you do to my house last night?" He was forced to add a begrudging 'thank you' as she slid a mug of coffee in front of him.

"The children love the decorations," Carol said.

He followed her gaze as she watched the children through the window. Hillary and Patrick had abandoned their snowman to start a good natured snowball fight.

"They are precious children."

"Thank you," Ben was forced to say again. As upset about the mess in the other room as he was, he couldn't be churlish enough to ignore her compliment. They were wonderful children. All the more reason to protect them from this holiday nonsense before it led to disappointment on a massive scale.

He picked up his coffee mug but froze when it was two inches from his lips. He'd never seen this mug before in his life. It was white and he moved it back so he could read what the red letters spelled out.

BE NICE! Or you'll end up on Santa's naughty list.

HE SLAMMED THE MUG DOWN, not caring that coffee sloshed onto the table. "Miss Kane, this has gone too far. Where are my coffee mugs?"

"On the top shelf of the pantry until after Christmas," she answered, apparently not at all rattled by his frustration. "I have others if you'd prefer." She rose and reached for his mug. "Let me get you a top-off. I have a Rudolph mug or you can have-"

"Sit down," he insisted. "Just what is the matter with you?"

She didn't sit. She stood, hands on her hips, the first crack in her calm composure beginning to show. "I could well ask you the same thing."

He stood and stared down at her. Her blue eyes snapped and a faint redness stained her cheeks. He pushed away the thought that she looked downright charming when she was angry. And she was angry. He could see it.

"This Christmas nonsense has to stop. Now."

"It isn't nonsense." She lifted her chin, defiance replacing her anger. "You're trying so hard to ruin our Christmas and I can't figure out why. It's you who should cease and desist with the scrooge routine."

Our Christmas? His head started to spin. Had she even been here a full twenty-four hours? Suddenly it was 'our' Christmas? That was going too far.

"I won't have my children subjected to lie after lie about someone who doesn't exist."

She narrowed her eyes at him. "Santa Claus does exist. You are the one spreading venomous lies with that book you're writing."

He froze. How did she know about his book?

"How did you-" but the rest of his question was cut off by the sound of the front door slamming open.

"Daddy, Miss Kane, come quickly," Hillary shouted. "It's Patrick. He needs help."

With Carol only a step behind him, Ben followed his daughter out the front door and down the front steps. Hillary pointed up to the roof where a frightened looking Patrick stood, a string of lights in hand.

"What happened," Ben asked Hillary. "Is he hurt?"

"He's stuck." Tears pooled in her eyes. "He's scared. He can't get down."

"You're alright, son," Ben called up, hoping his voice would reassure his son. "I'll have you down in a jiffy." Just how he had no idea. He'd donated his tall ladder and had meant to replace it, but hadn't gotten around to it. He swore under his breath.

"How did Patrick get up there?" Carol asked.

"He pretended he was a monkey, just like you said."

Ben shot an accusing look in Carol's direction but she didn't look at him. She looked up at Patrick.

"Patrick," she called out, "what are you doing up there?"

The little boy gulped. "I wanted to lay some lights on the roof for Santa. He needs a landing strip so he can land his sleigh."

"Damn." Ben clenched his good hand into a fist. "Do you see what you've done, Miss Kane?" he demanded. "All of this Santa nonsense is confusing the children."

He watched as Carol slowly turned to look at him. "It would seem that if you are comfortable enough to insult me and accuse me of bogus charges, then you should be comfortable enough to call me Carol." She turned away from him before he could respond.

"Patrick," she called, "I think that is a wonderful idea. I'm coming up to help you finish it and then we'll come down together, okay?"

The little boy nodded. "Can you hurry, Miss Kane? I'm afraid."

"I'll be right there, sweetie. Just hold on." She turned to Ben. "Talk to him until I get up there. Do your best to reassure him."

Before he could ask just how she planned to get up on the roof, Carol ran into the house. He and Hillary had barely begun to reassure Patrick before he saw Carol come around the other side of the chimney. He blinked in surprise.

He watched as Carol knelt down to hug Patrick. She must have said something to him that he couldn't hear because Ben saw his son nod in agreement.

"Look, Daddy," Hillary beamed. "Isn't Miss Kane clever? She's going to help Patrick make a landing spot for Santa." She grinned at her father. "Isn't she something special?"

"Oh, yes, she's something all right." How on earth had she gotten up there? As annoyed as he still was with her, Ben had to give her credit for saving the moment. She'd allowed Patrick to salvage his pride by finishing what he'd gone up on the roof to do. To a little boy, being able to save face was no small thing.

"We're done," Carol called down. She pulled a small camera from her pocket and snapped a photo of a now proud looking Patrick standing in front of his design. She then returned to the edge. "Hillary, please stand under the tree and talk to Patrick as he comes down. He's going to demonstrate that at heart, he truly is a monkey."

Ben watched with pride as Patrick stepped forward, took a deep breath and reached out for the branch. He joined Hillary in distracting Patrick as he slowly made his way down. As soon as his son's feet touched the ground Ben pulled his son close and hugged him.

"We have to help Miss Kane get down now," Hillary reminded them.

Ben glanced up. Carol wasn't anywhere in sight. "Where did she go?"

Patrick shrugged. "Around the back of the chimney, the same way she came up."

They all three turned when they heard the front door close. Carol, now wearing her red wool coat and matching beret, locked the front door and came to stand beside them. Ben saw that she had his down jacket over her arm.

She handed it to him. "Are we ready?"

Ben was almost afraid to ask. "For what?"

"We're going to the mall."

Obviously not the least bit traumatized by the roof escapade, Hillary and Patrick let out a shout of joy and ran toward the SUV. Ben didn't budge.

"Why on earth would you want to go to the mall?" he demanded.

"To show you just how wrong you are." She lifted an eyebrow in challenge. "Santa is real and I can prove it."

He stared at her. The woman was insane, or at least teetering on the edge of insanity.

Or perhaps he was the one who was insane for allowing her to live in the same house with his children. Except that she was wonderful with them. He'd never seen his son or daughter look so happy. So carefree. So much like normal children. Carol Kane would make the perfect nanny. She was, he suddenly realized, exactly what they needed in their lives.

Carol stood next to the SUV, motioning for him to get in the passenger side. "Hurry up, Mr. Hanson. We don't want to keep Santa Claus waiting. This is his busy season after all."

Ben felt suddenly energized. Focused. The solution was obvious. All he had to do was help Carol get over her ridiculous obsession with Christmas.

CHAPTER 6

The Indian Village Mall parking lot was overflowing with cars. It took six trips through the entire lot to finally find a spot. Carol tried to ignore Ben's grumbling as she held his car door open for him. He was Beyond Bah Humbug personified. She seriously doubted he'd had any trouble coming up with the title for his book.

Her mood improved greatly as they neared the mall entrance. Christmas music blared from the speakers and the outside of the building was bedecked in festive green and red trim with silver giant bells. When they entered the three story atrium area she stopped short. "Oh, look, kids, it's just like home."

Hillary and Patrick, each with one mitten clad hand in hers, glanced up at her, matching quizzical expressions on their faces.

"For Santa, I mean. It must feel so like home for Santa," she quickly corrected herself. She ignored Ben's eyes on her. His watchful gaze was disconcerting. Had she given herself away? No, of course not. If he didn't believe in Santa, then he would never believe that Santa had a daughter.

She and the children circled the North Pole display several times, oohing and aahing over the toy workshop. Fourteen elves carved, chiseled and hammered away at wooden toys. Fourteen. Ha. Fourteen hundred was more like it, and even with that number they were barely hitting their quota on time. It also struck her as funny that the workshop area was so neat and orderly. This close to the twenty-fifth the elves would be ankle deep in scraps of wrapping paper and ribbons. Wading through the chaotic workroom invariably meant she'd find scotch tape on the bottoms of her shoes. She smiled.

"I like it too," Hillary beamed. "Thank you for bringing us, Miss Kane."

Carol smiled down at her. She loved the joyful sparkle in Hillary's eyes. This was what Christmas was truly about. Now she just needed to get Mr. Humbug to wake up and recognize it. To her surprise, she realized just how much she liked Ben Hanson. He was handsome, intelligent, kind and, if you didn't count his bias against seasonal joy, he was a wonderful father.

"Oh, and thank you too, Daddy," Hillary added.

Ben shook his head. "Trust me, the idea was all Miss Kane's."

Carol glanced over at him. If he'd had the use of

both arms she had no doubt he'd have them crossed over his chest in a sulky protest.

"So, are we ready to meet Santa?" she asked the children.

A delighted chorus of yeses was exactly the response she'd hoped for. "Let's go then. The line starts over there." She pointed to the end of a line that started at the entrance to the North Pole and snaked around the side of the display where animated penguins skated around an igloo. She quickly counted the people in line ahead of them as they took their position at the end. Only thirteen families in front of them. Not bad for this time of year.

"Good God, Carol, there has to be at least ten families ahead of us." Ben ran his good hand through his hair. She tried to ignore how roguishly attractive he looked with tousled hair. His churlish attitude, on the other hand, was comparatively much easier for her to disregard.

"Thirteen, actually."

He groaned.

She turned and looked up into his brown eyes. "You have something more important to do this morning than spend time with your children?" Her tone, although challenging, stopped just short of rude. "Your book won't be out in time for this Christmas so you have months to work on it. It can wait."

He narrowed his eyes. "How do you know about my book?"

She paused for a long moment. "Your mother told me about it."

His eyes instantly widened. "My mother? You spoke to my mother? When?"

"Last night. She phoned again after you were asleep." Carol had rather enjoyed her conversation with Ben's mother. Much like Ben's sister, his mother seemed a very reasonable and perfectly pleasant person. Ben must take after his father. "We had a perfectly lovely conversation."

"About my book?" His voice sounded strained. His shoulder must bother him more than he wanted to admit.

Carol shrugged. "We talked about it enough to know it's ridiculous. The whole premise is entirely negative. What good can come of spreading a false-hood with the sole intention of taking away people's joy?"

"What falsehood?" His brow was furrowed. "That Santa is a myth?"

"Sshh...lower your voice." She looked around to see if anyone was paying them any mind. "There are children around."

He rolled his eyes. "You're...you're just...just so..." he stopped when he saw that his son and daughter were looking up at him expectantly.

"Miss Kane is so what, Daddy?" Patrick asked. "So nice?"

"Yes, of course she's nice," he conceded.

"So pretty too, don't you think?" Hillary chimed in.

Carol felt her face flush as Ben's eyes roved over her. After a long moment she looked away.

"Miss Kane is very pretty," he finally said, his voice a bit softer now.

She still kept her eyes averted from his. They all moved up in line as another family went into Santa's inner sanctum. Thank heaven the line was moving.

"What do we say to Santa?" Patrick asked.

Carol opened her mouth to answer him but Ben spoke first.

"Listen, kids, we need to get this straight right now. There is no Santa Claus."

Carol cringed. Ben's voice was entirely too loud and far too adamant. This wasn't either the time or place. She shook her head, desperately trying to signal him to be quiet but he ignored her.

"Santa Claus is a lie," he went on. "It's nothing more than a story parents make up to control their children's behavior for one month out of every year. In fact-"

His next words were drowned out by the sound of crying children. And angry parents. Voices were raised, nasty looks were aplenty and Carol was sure that the woman behind them wanted to physically harm Ben but instead she settled for hissing at him, "I hope there's a coal mine in your stocking, you Grinch."

Carol's heart sank. This was a disaster. And it was at least half her fault. She should have known he wasn't ready for a visit yet.

"Elf coming through, excuse me, elf coming through," a voice called as families stepped to the side to make room for one of Santa's helpers. "Pardon me, please."

As the voice grew nearer, Carol's heart leapt. It was Jolly.

"It seems there's a situation here," Jolly said once she stood before them. The elf gave no indication she recognized Carol. "Anything I can help with?"

Carol waved her hand in Ben's direction. "We have a non-believer here."

It didn't escape her notice that Ben had the good grace to flush but he, wisely she thought, remained silent.

Jolly looked up at Ben and made a tsking sound. "We can't have that. I think you'd better come with me."

"Where?" Ben asked.

"Wherever Santa wants you to go," Carol said.

"Now, that's just enough, Carol." Ben's voice grew louder. "You have to stop this Christmas nonsense. The children find you enchanting. I see why, but this fixation on Santa is just going overboard. It's too much. It's all going to end in misery for everyone."

"If you don't stop grousing then yes, I agree, you're going to make us all miserable," Carol said. She turned her back on him, focusing her attention on the shrinking line in front of them. She was only four families away from seeing her father. That was enough to keep her tears of frustration at bay. Ben Hanson was too much. She couldn't take any more of this. And she wasn't too proud to beg her father to let her go back to the North Pole with him. She couldn't do any good here.

She steadfastly refused to turn around despite the fact that Ben was now quarrelling with the woman in line behind them. She felt Patrick slip his hand in hers and squeeze it gently. She squeezed it back. Patrick tugged on her arm. She bent down.

"Do you want to leave, sweetie?" she asked. Ben's boorish behavior was so unfair to the children.

"No, I want to see Santa. But I need to tell you something."

"I'm listening, Patrick."

"Daddy has trouble being happy. Please don't be mad at him."

Carol stared down at the boy. His wide eyes begged her to understand. She nodded. "I'll try not to be mad with your father, Patrick. I promise." She blew out a long breath. This was a promise she needed to keep. Her father was right. Patrick was right. Ben needed her help. "We'll all help your father learn to love Christmas."

Patrick's wide smile warmed her heart. She took a deep breath and turned back around to placate Ben. One glance at Jolly's face was all she needed to know that Ben was still going at it. She felt Patrick nudge her forward as yet another lucky family got into see Santa. Three families and counting.

"Mr. Hanson, I really think it's time to take a deep breath," Carol suggested.

"I think the elf wants Daddy to apologize," Hillary said.

"For what?" Ben's expression was incredulous. "For telling the truth? For denouncing a lie that parents perpetuate for no reason other than to-"

The appearance of a beefy security guard signaled that Ben's tirade was coming to an end soon. One way or another. "Ma'am," he addressed Carol. "I'm going to ask your husband here to step out of line with me."

Hillary wasted no time in setting the record straight. "Oh, they're not married. She's just moved in with us but my Dad hardly knows her. Isn't that right, Miss Kane?"

"Umm…." Carol's mind raced to find a suitable response. "Technically, that's true."

"So he's not your husband?" the guard clarified.

"No, he's not," she admitted.

"Lucky miss," the woman behind Ben said, drawing a few laughs from the crowd. "I'd suggest you move out while you still can."

Ben flushed. "I'm not budging until my kids have a chance to see this Santa fellow."

"Look, mister, I'm not letting you get anywhere near the Big Guy." He reached out for Ben's good arm but Ben moved aside.

"Touch me and I'm calling the police." Ben narrowed his eyes and stared at the guard.

"Saves me a call," the guard shot back.

"Stop, stop, stop…please," Carol begged. She smiled encouragingly at the guard. "Please let us just see Santa.

The children are so excited." She waited hopefully as he looked at Hillary and then Patrick. Just as she thought, their adorable faces did the trick.

"Okay, but only because you're at the front of the line now." He shook his head and sighed deeply before addressing Ben. "Not another word or I'm escorting you out of here." He turned to Carol. "I'll be right over there, Ma'am." He pointed to a spot a few feet away.

Carol smiled her thanks. She ushered the children to the front of the line and then put her hand on Ben's back and gave him a tiny shove forward.

"We can ask Santa for anything we want?" Patrick asked.

She nodded and smiled. "Anything. Santa's a great listener."

Hillary and Patrick put their little heads together for a last minute conference. Carol looked up at Ben. To his credit, his expression was sheepish.

"Don't get your hopes up, Mr. Hanson," Carol said. "That was coal worthy behavior back there."

He sighed. "Ben. Just call me Ben."

She raised an eyebrow and fixed him with as stern a look as she could muster. "Okay, Ben, not one negative word out of you while we're in there."

He nodded.

Jolly motioned them forward. "Your turn now, Santa's ready to see you."

Finally.

CHAPTER 7

Despite her delight at seeing her father, Carol managed not to throw herself into his arms. Christmas magic was always about children, first and foremost. She gave Hillary and Patrick a gentle push forward. She did, however, smile widely when her father winked at her.

"Who do we have here?" Santa asked. He motioned for them to come forward. When they stood before him, suddenly shy, he reached out and shook their hands in return. "Don't tell me, I know who you are! You're Hillary and Patrick Hanson."

The children exchanged wide eyed glances and turned back to Santa, nodding enthusiastically.

"That's us," Hillary said.

Patrick continued to stare, apparently unable to speak. Hillary elbowed him.

"How are you Santa?" he finally came out with.

Carol's father grinned broadly. "You're a good boy

to ask, thank you very much. I'm fine. A bit busy this time of year, but you know that."

Both children nodded.

Carol heard Ben choke back what was doubtless a smart remark. She turned and glared at him. She should have let the security guard take him to a gray, windowless little room to wait until they were done with their visit. She shook her head at him, doing her best to warn him to be quiet.

He had the good grace to look away.

"Now, let me think," Santa said, stroking his beard. He looked at Hillary first. "I have heard from your teacher, Mrs. Gonzalez, that you've been a wonderful student this year. She says you're bright, helpful, and kind to the other children. Is that so?"

Hillary nodded solemnly and then turned to look at her father and Carol. Her eyes shone with a delighted pride that touched Carol's heart. She smiled encouragingly at her. Hillary turned back around to face Santa. Carol snuck a glance at Ben. There was no way he could witness his daughter's delight and not be as touched as she was. He was frowning but it was a different kind of frown. Less disapproving and more perplexed. Maybe there was hope for him yet.

Santa reached out and placed a hand on Hillary's head. "I'm proud of you, my girl. The world needs more people as good hearted as you are."

"Thank you, Santa."

"Now," he continued, "tell me what you'd most like for Christmas."

"May we ask you for two things, Santa? One is for Patrick and me, and one is for...for someone else."

"Go right ahead," he answered.

"Well, we'd love a puppy. One that will grow into a big shaggy dog like you see in the movies."

Ben groaned. "Hillary, that is out of the question-" but he stopped speaking when Santa held up a gloved hand.

"A puppy? Hmmm...I hadn't thought of that. Is this what you'd like too, Patrick?" He turned to the boy. "Would you enjoy having a puppy?"

In answer, Patrick burst into tears. Carol and Ben both rushed forward.

"It's okay, honey." Carol knelt down and rubbed his back.

"Look what you've done," Ben glared at Santa. "Your interrogations are terrorizing my son."

Patrick shook his head vehemently. "No, Daddy."

Ben looked perplexed. "Then what's wrong son?"

"I'm not sad. I'm happy." Patrick said, hiccups rapidly replacing his tears. "I never imagined we could have a dog of our own, especially a big slobbery one. It's like I'm having the best dream ever."

Carol shot a triumphant look at Ben. She hoped that her father came through big time on this one. She wished she could help him scour the world for a dog that would do nothing but shed on the furniture, chew on shoes, and drive Ben crazy. It was no less than he deserved.

"I need to talk to Mrs. Claus about this because

puppies, kittens, and ponies are her department," Santa told the children. "But my wife is soft hearted so I'd suggest that you start thinking of names in case there is a furry creature under your Christmas tree."

Both children jumped up and down and clapped their hands, their enthusiastic squeals drowning out Ben's protests.

"Now, what else was it that you wanted to ask me for my dear?" Santa prompted Hillary.

"We would like it if you could help Daddy to like Miss Kane as much as we do."

"Oh, I see," Santa nodded understandingly. "You both like Miss Kane, do you?"

"Ever so much," Hillary said. Patrick nodded. "We'd like her to stay with us forever."

Silence filled Santa's inner sanctum. Carol met her father's eyes. She'd never seen him look so uncertain, and to save her life, she couldn't think of a single thing to say to help him out.

"Okay, that's quite enough," Ben spoke first. He swooped down and took his son's hand in his. "Children, say goodbye to...to, um, Mr. Claus." After they did as he bid, he ushered them toward the exit. He glanced back over his shoulder at Carol. "Are you coming?"

She shook her head. "You go ahead, I'd like a word with Santa."

"Oh, for crying out loud, Carol, can we just stop this charade?"

They stood a few feet apart, yet worlds away in

belief, and stared at each other. Carol couldn't speak. To know that Ben was incapable of believing in something as essentially good as Santa made her heart hurt. Her father saved her from having to speak.

"Goodbye, Mr. Hanson, and Merry Christmas," Santa said. His voice was still gentle for the children's sake but it also held an unmistakable air of authority. "Miss Kane will be with you shortly, so kindly wait outside." He then bade the children goodbye in a more cheerful voice.

After Ben and the children left, Santa stood and held out his arms. Carol hugged him tightly, grateful to have a moment alone with him.

"Oh, Daddy, I'm so confused."

"It seems you aren't the only one," he said. He kissed her on the top of her head before he held her at arm's length and looked thoughtfully at her. "This appears to be more of a challenge than I'd realized."

Carol nodded, suddenly unable to follow through on her plan to beg her father to take her home. It wasn't time to go back to the North Pole.

"I don't know what I should do next," Carol confessed. "Or what I'm doing wrong."

"You're doing everything right, honey. That's why Mr. Hanson is so rattled. You're making progress."

Carol didn't think so. But she'd never argued with her father before and wasn't about to start now.

"Now, this Ben of yours is a tough nut to crack, that's for sure," Santa said. "So I think you should go hard core."

"Can you be a bit more specific?" She actually wanted more than specific, she wanted a full-blown plan of attack broken down into five easy steps.

"You don't have much time," her father conceded. "So I suggest you put him on a diet of candy canes and eggnog, plenty of cookies and milk too. Keep the Christmas music going 24/7 and here," he dug into a pocket of his velvet jacket, "you might as well get him to wear this."

Carol took the folded fabric square and looked at it questioningly.

"It's a reindeer patterned sling that your mother made for him," he said in answer to her unspoken question. "She feels sorry for him."

Carol groaned. "And what do you think of him?"

Her father gave a half smile. "He has potential. But the real question is this, what do you think of him?"

Carol kept her eyes on the sling in her hands. She didn't want to put her feelings into words. Besides, her father knew. If he knew when girls and boys around the world had been nice, and when they'd been naughty, he certainly knew his own daughter's heart. She looked up at him, and the tender expression in his eyes assured her that he knew. She sighed.

"Carol, honey, I believe in you. If it helps, just focus on enjoying the holiday and encouraging Ben to enjoy it with you."

He said that like it was an easy thing. She reached up and kissed his cheek. "I'll do my best, Daddy." With one last hug, she headed toward the exit but turned around when a question popped into her mind. "How is Nicholas holding up without me there? Is he getting the job done?"

Santa shook his head, a playful smile on his lips. "Let's just say it was a good thing that boy wasn't twins."

"SHE KISSED SANTA. I SAW HER."

Ben looked at his son in disbelief. First the happy tears over a puppy there wasn't a snowball's chance in hell he was going to get, and now this story.

"Patrick doesn't lie, Daddy," Hillary chimed in. She put a protective arm around her brother's shoulder. "You asked him to peek in Santa's room and he's only telling you what he saw."

"Of course, I'm sorry, son. I believe you." But of course he didn't. The poor child was under the spell of a tall tale spun into a commercially overrun holiday. He actually shared his son's disorientation. Ever since Carol had arrived, charming and cheery, he'd felt like his grasp on reality was tenuous at best.

"What did she say? Did you hear anything?" Ben couldn't stop himself from asking.

"Daddy! You can't spy on Santa!" Hillary's frown was the most ferocious he'd ever seen. "You'll ruin our chances of getting a puppy."

"There's not going to be a puppy-" he broke off when he saw Carol emerge from Santa's lair and walk toward them. What the heck kind of pain killers had the doctor given him? Something wasn't right. His heart was beating way too fast.

"What is that look for?" Carol's voice broke through his thoughts.

Ben started, embarrassed to be caught staring at her, but then he realized she was looking at his children.

"Daddy said we can't have a puppy," Patrick said.

"Daddy's not in charge of puppies," Hillary added. "That's Santa Claus's department, isn't it, Miss Kane?"

"Technically my...Mrs. Claus is in charge of those decisions," Carol said. "But we do need to discuss this further at home," she continued.

At home. Ben felt a stab of envy for any man fortunate enough to share a home, children, and a life with Carol. Hillary and Patrick meant everything to him. He was also grateful to have a secure job and safe home to raise his children in. But the woman before him, the one holding hands with his children, the one patiently explaining the responsibility involved in owning a pet, wasn't his.

He heard Carol's voice through his thoughts. "Are you okay, Ben?"

He blinked twice. He had to get a grip or he was heading straight into a world of trouble he'd didn't need. Might want. But didn't need. He shook his head. Christmas was making him crazy.

"Daddy's fine." Hillary smiled up at him.

He smiled back.

"He's just upset you kissed Santa," she added.

He stopped smiling. He glanced at Carol. "Did you?"

Her eyes widened. "Did I what?"

"Kiss Santa Claus?"

She opened her mouth and then closed it again without answering him. He watched as a dozen emotions flitted across her face, none of which he could identify. When it came to women, he knew he couldn't decode their subtle body language and tricky word choices. He thought it safer to wait for her to speak.

"He's my father...my...he's Father Christmas," Carol sputtered, and her cheeks reddened.

This much body language he could read. He knew he should be quiet now. But all of the tension, frustration, and another emotion he refused to name, pushed him on. "Can you see how ridiculous this whole belief in Santa Claus is, Carol? Don't you see that you've bought into a story about an old man who-"

"Not another word," she practically hissed at him. She bent and spoke quietly to the children before walking rapidly toward the mall exit.

He watched her for a moment, caught off guard by her action. He jogged to catch up with them and fell in step beside her.

"Carol, stop, please. There's no shame in admitting the truth."

She stopped and whirled around to look up at him, her eyes flashing.

To save his life, he couldn't look away. Her chest

rose and fell with her rapid breathing and a strand of her dark hair fell into her eyes.

"Ben," she narrowed her eyes, "pay attention because this is non-negotiable. We're going home to spend the day eating candy cane ice cream, drinking hot chocolate, watching Miracle on 34th Street and then we'll read Christmas stories to the children. After they go to bed, I'm going to talk, and you're going to listen." She turned on her heel and strode off again.

Between the challenge he could see in Carol's eyes, and the way his heart hammered in his chest, Ben knew he was in trouble. Big trouble.

CHAPTER 8

Three classic Christmas movies, two pints of peppermint ice cream and one long evening later, Carol tucked her charges into their respective beds. Patrick, worn out from hours of unbridled fun, fell asleep as soon as his little head hit the pillow. His sister, on the other hand, looked pensive as Carol leaned down and kissed her forehead.

"And what are we looking so worried about?" Carol sat on the edge of the little girl's bed. "I thought you had fun tonight."

"Oh, I did." Hillary said.

"You're worried, aren't you?" Carol reached for her hand and gave it a reassuring squeeze. "Do you want to talk about it?"

Hillary nodded, but remained silent.

Carol waited patiently. Whatever it was that was bothering Hillary, she wanted to know about. She had a good idea what it was but she waited for the girl to speak.

"It's Daddy."

Just as Carol thought. She smiled encouragingly. "What about your father?"

"He's...he's...oh, Miss Kane, he's going to ruin Christmas." Her confession was followed by a torrent of tears.

Carol gathered Hillary into her arms, holding her close while she cried. She rubbed the little girl's back and rocked her ever so gently. At the same time her mind raced with uncharitable thoughts. But she pushed them aside. The Claus family creed was burned into her heart. Christmas was about children, first, foremost, and last.

Once Hillary appeared to be cried out, Carol helped her back into bed. "Better?"

After she nodded, Carol asked, "What are you really worried about?"

Hillary bit her lip. "I want Daddy to be happy, I do. But Patrick and I really want Santa to come. And he won't if Daddy keeps saying he doesn't exist."

"You can trust Santa to do the right thing." She reached over and pushed a stand of hair away from Hillary's eye. "Your father will come around."

"How do you know that?"

Carol smiled. "Lots of fathers are like yours, it's hard for them to relax and enjoy the magic of Christmas."

"Was your father like that too?"

She shook her head. "No. My father loves Christmas more than anyone I know. But I've met other fathers who think like yours. But you know what, sweetie, it's up to us to help him enjoy it. I think he just doesn't know how."

Hillary's smile was one of relief. "I hope you're right, Miss Kane."

"I am." And as frustrated with Ben as she was, Carol still felt compelled to defend him. "You know, your dad is pretty great in every other way, isn't he?"

Hillary nodded. "I think so." She yawned. "I'm so glad you're here with us, Miss Kane."

"I'm glad too." She patted the girl's hand and crossed to the door. She turned out the light switch. "Sweet dreams, honey."

"Miss Kane?"

"Yes?"

"I love Daddy," Hillary said, her voice now heavy with sleepiness.

"I know you do," Carol said. There was a lot to love about Ben Hanson. She pressed her hand against her chest but it did little to relieve the ache there. "He's a good man."

"You'll talk to Daddy? About Christmas?"

Carol didn't hesitate to reassure her. "Yes, Hillary. I'll do it right now."

BEN'S ARM ACHED, his head buzzed from a combination of too many sappy movies and two much sugar laden ice cream, and his jaw clenched every time he thought of the children's excitement about the idea of a puppy. A puppy? Was there no end to the commotion that Carol caused in his house? In his mind? In his heart?

He groaned and leaned his head back against the sofa cushions. He draped his good arm across his forehead. Maybe if he shut his eyes and counted to ten he'd wake up to find the whole thing had been merely a dream. He closed his eyes and counted slowly before opening them again. No. His living room still looked like a close-out sale at a Christmas in July store. All that was missing from the chaos was a puppy. A shoe chewing, un-house broken, hyperactive ball of fur. He closed his eyes again.

"What the hell was Santa thinking?" he muttered aloud.

"So you admit he does exist? That's progress."

Ben started to stand but Carol sat down on the sofa next to him before he could get up. He glanced over, knowing he should avoid eye contact. Hell, any kind of contact. But he couldn't resist. She was beautiful. And charming. And warm hearted. And intelligent. But most of all, she was trouble.

"The children are asleep," she told him. "Now we need to get down to business."

He shifted so that he was facing her. "If this is about the puppy, it's going to be a short conversation."

Her eyes flashed. A sure sign she was getting ready for battle, he thought. If he were smart he'd put a stop to this right now. He opened his mouth but she cut him off.

"Your daughter is afraid you're going to ruin Christmas." Carol raised an eyebrow expectantly and waited for him to speak.

His heart felt like it dropped twelve stories. "She said that?"

Carol nodded.

Ben couldn't remember a time where he'd felt so miserable. He loved his children. Heaven knew he was floundering trying to parent them alone, but he loved them. And he was screwing up big time if they didn't trust him not to ruin the holiday.

"After all you've been through these last few years I don't entirely blame you-"

"Blame me?" he interrupted her. "Me? You're the one who has turned Christmas into a nightmare."

He watched as her eyes widened. He decided to take full advantage of her very uncharacteristic speechlessness. "Before you came here we were fine," he continued. "The children had low, and I might add, realistic expectations of the holiday." He held up a finger to forestall the torrent of Christmas rhetoric that she looked about to let loose. "So if anyone around here is in danger of ruining anything, it's you."

Ben waited for an explosion. But none came. Instead, Carol sat looking at him, her anger replaced with a look of...what was it? Frustration? Not exactly. Pity? God, he hoped not. Sadness? Whatever it was, she didn't look happy and it was his fault.

He reached out. She moved back, not taking her eyes from his.

"Carol," he swallowed hard against the lump in his throat, "you have to understand where I'm coming from."

"I do." Her voice was quiet, steady. "I think I understand perfectly well."

He frowned. "You do?"

She nodded. "I understand that you're afraid to be happy. You're afraid to let your children be happy in some misguided attempt to keep them from being hurt. And you're taking it even further, writing your stupid book so that other parents will think they're parenting responsibly by withholding joy from their children." She shook her head. "All because you don't want to get hurt again."

He wanted to turn away from her. He needed to turn away from her if he was going to keep any shred of dignity or self-respect but he didn't. He couldn't. "It's not what you think."

"Isn't it?"

Her eyes searched his. He felt exposed in a way he never had before. No one had ever looked at him, truly seen him, the way that Carol now did. Vulnerable didn't begin to describe how he felt.

"Ben, you've been hurt. First your late wife was going to move out, and then she got sick and passed away. I know." Carol bit her lip and paused for a long moment. "But do you really think the answer is to teach Hillary and Patrick to stand on the sidelines of life so they won't get hurt?"

He looked away.

"Look at me, Ben," Carol said, and when he didn't she placed her hand on his good arm.

He closed his eyes against the warmth of her touch. He didn't want that warmth to reach his heart. Because when it was gone, when she was gone, he didn't think he could bear the cold.

They sat, surrounded by deafening silence. Ben felt at war with himself, it was unlike anything he'd ever experienced before. He knew what he wanted. Carol. Her enthusiasm, her charm, her kindness, her warmth...he wanted it all. But he knew if he let her into his life it would come at a price he didn't want to pay when she decided to leave. He couldn't do it. He couldn't experience true happiness only to have it taken away again.

He turned to face her. "I think it's better if you go."

She stared up at him for an agonizingly long moment before she nodded, understanding clear in her eyes. "I can get a flight out tomorrow night. After the party, but if that's not soon enough I can-"

"That's fine," he interrupted her. "Hillary and Patrick will want you here for it." The cursed, confounded party they'd told him about on the way home from the mall.

"You're sure?"

Her voice was so quiet he could barely hear her.

"Of course, the house is big enough that we can manage. It's only a few people over for cookies, right?"

She looked away.

"Carol?" He struggled to keep his voice level. "What aren't you telling me?"

She took a deep breath. That couldn't be a good sign.

"We're going to have a house full of people, aren't we?" he demanded.

She nodded.

Damn. All he wanted was to be alone in a dark house. No Christmas music, no strings of lights, no bell shaped cookies. And definitely no happy, cheerful people who wanted to make merry.

"The children are looking forward to this, Ben."

"I know, I know." He closed his eyes. He needed to do the right thing by his children, even if he was incapable of making a woman happy. "I'll get through it."

"I'm sorry."

It tore at his heart to hear how contrite she sounded, especially when it was all his fault. He'd railed at her about the holiday ever since she'd arrived but she'd done nothing wrong except make his children extremely happy. The fact he'd fallen in love with her and now wanted nothing more than forever with her was on his head, not hers.

"You have nothing to apologize for, Carol. I just don't...I just can't...," he let his voice trail off.

"You just don't believe."

"No, I don't," he conceded. "Not in any of it."

He watched as Carol left the room, waiting until he heard her bedroom door close before he switched off the light and sat in the dark. No. He didn't believe. Not in Christmas. And not in happy endings.

CHAPTER 9

"Come on sleepyhead, wake up."

In protest, Carol rolled over and refused to open her eyes. But that didn't stop someone from shaking her, or from scolding her, for that matter.

"For the love of Santa," the voice intoned, "get out of that bed. It's the day before Christmas Eve and you are not spending it laying around feeling sorry for yourself."

Ah, this was where the voice was completely wrong. Carol had every intention of feeling sorry for herself all day long. In fact, she had the ultimate pity party planned. And it was a party for one. "Go away."

"You would do this to your father, Carol, this late in December?"

Carol groaned. Guilt always worked. Especially so near the red letter day. She sat up, hugged her pillow to her chest and frowned at Jolly. "Don't you have things to do at the North Pole?"

The elf raised an eyebrow. "You know I do." She pulled the blankets from the bed and motioned for Carol to get out of it. "Your father sent me."

Carol stood barefoot on the cold wood floor and watched her friend make the bed. She and Jolly were fast friends, it was only two days before Christmas, and today was the Hanson's big party. These were things that normally would have made her happy. Yet she felt strangely detached from it all.

Jolly pointed to the pillow Carol was still holding. "Plump that up and put it with the others," she said. She waited until Carol did as she bid before speaking again. "Aren't you going to ask me how things are at home?"

"Of course, I'm sorry. How are things at home?"

"Thoughtful of you to ask." Jolly hoisted herself up to sit on the edge of the bed, her legs dangling over the edge. She pulled two candy canes from her pocket and offered one to Carol. When she refused, Jolly shook her head ruefully. "Wow, you must have it bad."

Carol sat next to her. "I do." She sighed. Ben Hanson had gotten to her in the worst way. He was all she could think about. But this wouldn't do. She had to snap out of it. "Now, I'm asking because I really want to know. How is everyone at home?"

"Well, when I left a few hours ago your father was poring over weather reports. I'm happy to say that the national weather service hasn't reported anything the Big Guy can't handle. Your mother is busy, busy, busy."

"And loving every moment of it," Carol interjected.

Jolly nodded. "She's in her element, that's for sure. Now your brother, that's a whole different story. Wanna hear the juicy details?"

Carol nodded.

"Nicholas was in so far over his head after you left that your father actually hired him a full-time assistant."

Carol's eyes widened. "No."

Jolly nodded, a gleam in her eye. "Oh, yes he did. Her name is Holly and she is, so Rapz informs me, blindingly beautiful. And smart. And she can run circles around your brother in the organization department. You see where this going?"

Carol grinned. "Oh, what I wouldn't give to witness that in person."

"Just what I wanted to hear you say. Let's get you packed." Jolly hopped off the side of the bed and opened the closet door.

"What are you talking about?" Carol ran around the side of the bed and reached over Jolly's head to close the closet. "I'm not leaving."

"Oh, yes you are," Jolly shot back.

A strange panicky feeling ran through Carol. "I haven't even wrapped the presents yet."

"That's your only objection to going home?" Jolly asked. "Because I can do that while you pack. I'm no Rapz but I am fast. So, if that's it..." her voice trailed off knowingly.

"Well, it's just that I haven't...we haven't...well, I

can't explain it." She couldn't explain her reluctance to leave because she didn't understand it herself.

"Maybe you can't, but I can," Jolly told her. "It's pretty obvious what's going on around here." She slid the closet door open and pulled out Carol's suitcase. "Start packing. The Big Guy wants you home."

"What?"

Jolly took a deep breath and spoke in an exaggeratedly slow voice. "Your father, known to all the world as Santa Claus, wants you to come home with me."

"Today?" Carol's heart began to race. She hadn't expected this, but maybe she should have. She'd failed in her mission and of course, Santa knew.

"Can I get some help here?" Jolly's voice broke through her thoughts.

Carol glanced at the suitcase and then reluctantly lifted it onto the bed and plopped down beside it. "But I'm not ready to go."

"Yes, I can see how unbelievably happy you are here." Jolly shook her head. "You've accomplished what your father wanted of you and now it's time to go back."

"That's just it, Jolly. I haven't accomplished anything." Carol buried her face in her hands. Facing her father would be hard. Saying goodbye to Patrick and Hillary would be miserable. And knowing that she would never see Ben Hanson again was torture.

"We've had a miscommunication, I see," Jolly said. "Because Santa told me this morning that your work here was done and I was to bring you home."

Carol shook her head. She couldn't feel more miserable that she'd let her father down. "He just said that because he knows I can't do what he wanted me to."

"He said that because Mr. Bah Humbug deleted his book and all of his notes from his hard drive last night. Right after you went to bed, from what I understand."

Carol stared at her friend, hardly daring to hope she'd heard that right. "You mean it? Ben actually did that?"

Jolly nodded, a triumphant little smile on her face. "So it looks like you got under his skin as much as he got under yours. Now, let's pack."

"Wait, Jolly, I can't leave now." Carol stood, feeling suddenly invigorated by the news. "I have to at least stay for the party." She just wanted the one evening to celebrate the holiday with Ben and the children. "Surely that's not too much to ask?"

"Actually it is," Jolly held up a hand. "Nick is so beyond enamored with Holly that he can barely focus. Your parents are working too hard. Bottom line, we need you. Children around the world need you."

Carol shook her head and folded her arms across her chest in further protest. "These children need me here. I'm not leaving."

Jolly groaned. "Your father warned me that you would be stubborn about this."

"I belong here, Jolly." The truth resonated in Carol's heart as she said the words aloud. She belonged here. With the children. With Ben.

The elf massaged her temples and thought for a moment. "Okay, here's your final offer. You stay for the party, enjoy the heck out of it, and then tonight we go home. Santa wants you home for Christmas."

Carol's mind raced through her options. If she stayed for the party tonight and left for the North Pole with Jolly right afterwards then she'd be home to help for Christmas Eve. The twenty-fourth was an all hands on deck situation at the North Pole. She was good at her job and she wanted to be a part of the magic before she came back here.

"Do we have a deal?" Jolly asked.

Carol nodded. "Yes, I'll go home with you after the party."

Jolly smiled. "Great. Hit the shower then and I'll get you packed up."

AFTER SHOWERING and changing into a pair of black wool slacks and a black cashmere sweater, Carol ran lightly down the stairs. Hearing voices in the kitchen, she headed that way. But the sight that met her eyes upon entering the room caused her to stop short. In fact, it all but knocked the air out of her lungs.

"Hi Miss Kane!"

"Good morning Carol!"

She looked from Rapz to Hillary to Patrick and then back at Rapz. Her eyes widened even further as she surveyed the flour covered room. "What's going on here?"

It was Rapz who answered first. "The children are learning to bake."

Carol looked for an inch of counter space that wasn't covered in flour but couldn't find one. The mess, however, was less shocking than seeing the children happily making a disaster of the kitchen with one of Santa's helpers.

Her two worlds had just collided.

"Today? Why today?" She shook her head. "Never mind. Where's your father?" she asked. She needed to head Ben off at the pass.

"On the phone with a dog breeder," Hillary supplied. "We told him that Santa would take care of the puppy but Daddy said he thought he should make some calls just in case."

Rapz shook his head. "Personally, I'd let the Big Guy handle it."

Carol pinched herself. No. It wasn't a dream. Or a nightmare. Not yet.

She dashed into the hallway and hesitated, listening for Ben's voice. She didn't hear him but she saw that the front door was unlocked. Without bothering to grab a jacket, she stepped out onto the front porch.

When she closed the front door behind her, Ben spun around.

His smile made Carol's heart soar. He held the telephone in his good hand. She grinned when she saw he was wearing the sling his mother had made for him.

"Good morning," she said. "I heard you were trying to track down a puppy."

He nodded sheepishly. "Not having much luck though."

"Just leave it to Santa," Carol said.

His smile faded. "Carol, please, we don't have to pretend that Santa is real when the kids aren't around, okay?"

Carol stared at him, confused. "So you haven't changed your mind about Santa Claus?"

"Well, I have, in a way. And you're to thank for that. After we spoke last night I realized how happy the children were believing in the Santa myth. I mean, they're little for such a short amount of time, right? Why not let them indulge in a little harmless make believe?"

Harmless make believe. She shivered.

"Let's get you inside, you'll freeze out here." Ben stepped around her and opened the front door, guiding her into the foyer with a gentle hand on her back. "There, that heat feels much better."

Except that it didn't. Carol felt numb. "What about your book?"

"I'm shelving it for now."

"For now?" She'd been so very stupid to assume because he deleted his files that he had decided not to write his book.

He nodded. "You made me realize how much Hillary and Patrick need me to be actually present, and I'm not when I'm holed up in my study typing away. I still think Christmas is a crock and little better than a hoax, but this year I need to focus on my children. You've helped me see that." He reached out to stroke her cheek with his fingertips. "Thank you. For everything."

Carol couldn't think of a thing to say. Fortunately Ben didn't seem to expect her to because he wasn't done.

"I know I asked you to leave last night. I'm sorry, Carol. I panicked." He took her hand and lifted it to his lips. "You've changed everything around here. You've brought the kids such happiness and you've brought me," he touched his heart, "hope."

"Hope," she repeated dully. His word choice was ironic considering that she felt utterly hopeless right now.

"I was hoping we could talk tonight, after the party. About us."

"Us?"

He nodded, and ran his hand through his hair, suddenly looking slightly unsure of himself. "Yes, us. You. Me. Look, I don't want you to go. Not tonight. Not, well, not ever. But we can take it as slowly as you'd like. Just promise you'll cancel your flight tonight."

She nodded, but only to make this painful conversation stop.

Ben smiled. "Good. Now we'd better get into the kitchen and see what kind of mess my kids and your friends from the mall are making."

Friends from the mall? Oh, Jolly and Rapz. So he

had seen them, and obviously he'd recognized Jolly, but he must have assumed they were actors playing Santa's helpers. Just like he refused to believe her father was anything other than a retiree with a steady seasonal gig. She watched him walk into the kitchen. His willingness to ignore the obvious fact that there were two elves in his house was proof they belonged in two separate worlds.

Carol covered her face with her hands, willing away her tears. She'd get through the party for the children's sake. She'd act like her father's daughter and celebrate the season with a houseful of Ben's neighbors and co-workers.

But she wasn't going to cancel her flight. For when the evening was all over, and the house was clean and the children asleep, she'd be on the first sleigh back to the North Pole.

CHAPTER 10

"Oh, Miss Kane, isn't this the loveliest party ever?"

Carol ruffled Hillary's hair affectionately. "I'm glad you're enjoying it."

"Daddy seems to be too, don't you think?" Hillary asked, turning to look up at Carol. "He's talking to those men from the newspaper and he looks very relaxed."

"He certainly does." Carol decided that a swift change of subject was in order, because looking at, talking about, or even thinking about Ben made her sad. "How many people have told you how lovely you look?"

"I didn't think it was polite to count." Hillary grinned. "Eight."

Carol laughed and leaned down to hug the girl. When she stood she felt Ben's gaze on her but she refused to look directly at him. She'd managed to avoid contact with him all evening. With a house full of guests it had been easy to slip out of any room he entered. Also, the fact he knew everyone present meant he'd been waylaid by someone wanting to talk to him each time he'd tried to get close to her. She turned her attention back to Hillary. "It's been so very nice getting to know you and Patrick."

"Why do you sound like you're saying goodbye?" Hillary asked. Her little brow furrowed and she grabbed Carol's hand. "You're not leaving us, are you?"

Carol cursed her own stupidity. She'd been so wrapped up in her own heartache that she'd slipped. "No," she lied, "of course not. And leave you with all these dirty dishes to clean up? Never."

Mollified, Hillary went back to chatting about what the other guests were doing, saying and wearing. Carol only half listened. As sad as the thought made her, she was grateful that the elves had brought a bag of 'forget-me' dust that she could sprinkle over the children just before she left that night. They wouldn't miss her, or even remember her, which would make the last few days as if they'd never happened. A lump formed in Carol's throat and she was glad Hillary didn't appear to want her to do anything but listen.

She glanced at her watch. Less than three hours to go.

BEN REALIZED with a start that he was having a good

time, as in actually enjoying himself. He lifted his beer glass and took a slow sip, savoring not only its coldness but the magic of the moment. Across the room his son was playing with two neighbor kids, and not too far away his daughter stood hand in hand with Carol. Hillary looked happy. Just good old fashioned happy. The way children should look. And he owed it all to Carol.

He tried but couldn't catch her eye. He frowned. He'd probably scared her with his talk of having her stay forever. He didn't blame her for being over-whelmed by hosting a party for a houseful of people she'd never met, or by his spontaneous and ill-timed confession of his feelings for her. It was scary for him too. He'd never been open with his first wife, but then he hadn't felt the way about her that he felt about Carol. He felt sure this time. Absolutely sure they were meant to be together.

He looked down at his watch. Two hours and fifty minutes, by then he was certain the house would be empty, the children on their way to bed, and he and Carol could begin to make plans for their future.

"ARE you sure you want to do this, Carol? There's no going back once we sprinkle them."

Carol nodded. "Go ahead, Jolly. We need to leave and this is easiest on the children." She stood back from Patrick's bed and watched as Jolly dipped her hand into the small green satin bag she'd brought from home. Jolly waved her hand over the little boy and a light fairy dusting of green and silver sparkles swirled over his head and then evaporated.

"When did we add silver?" Carol asked.

Jolly shrugged. "I don't know. You'll have to ask Rapz later. I haven't worked in the Christmas Magic department for almost a year now."

Carol straightened Patrick's blanket and blew him a kiss. He wouldn't remember her, but she'd never forget him.

Jolly tugged at her sleeve. "We have to do the same for the girl, come on."

They slipped across the hall into Hillary's room. She lay curled up under her blanket, her stuffed black lab puppy in her arms. At the end of her bed her faded pink tutu lay ready for the next day. Carol reached down and ran the satin ties through her fingers. She issued a swift but fervent prayer that both children would only ever know happiness. When she opened her eyes she nodded to give Jolly the go-ahead. It was for the best that Hillary not remember the last few days. With one last lingering glance at the little girl who'd found a permanent place in her heart, Carol followed Jolly into the hallway.

"Now, how do we administer this to Mr. Scrooge?" Jolly held up the bag and looked at Carol expectantly.

"Don't call him that." Carol bit her lip in thought. "You know, I think it's better if we don't give him any."

In answer, Jolly grabbed ahold of Carol's arm and

all but dragged her into the guest bedroom. Once the door was shut she let loose. "I knew, I knew it! You've got a thing for the anti-Christmas."

"Sssh…lower your voice," Carol said. "He's downstairs loading the dishwasher and I don't want him to hear us."

"You don't want him to forget you," Jolly corrected her. "Carol, you need to think this through before you leave. I can go back and tell Santa that-"

But Carol didn't let her finish the sentence. "No, Miss Know it All, you're way off the mark. I just don't want Ben to get a dose because then then he'll be right back to where he was a few days ago attitude wise. So, if we want the children to have a special Christmas then we leave Ben the way he is."

"Do you want to say good-bye to him?"

Carol shook her head. "It's better if we just leave." She took her suitcase in hand and pointed to the window. "If we go out this way, it's just a short jump to the roof."

"Lead the way," Jolly said.

Carol lifted up the window sash and swung a leg over the sill. A blast of cold night air hit her in the face just as the realization that she wouldn't see Ben or the children again hit her heart. She inhaled. The bite of cold in the air reminded her of home. Home. She needed to focus on where she belonged and not on where she wanted to be.

She swung her other leg over to stand on the ledge. She then tossed her suitcase above her head before she made the small leap to the rooftop, steadying herself before reaching down to help Jolly up. They only needed to wait a few moments before they heard the sound of sleigh bells approaching. When the sleigh touched down they hopped in and Jolly gave the order for them to head back to the North Pole. As they lifted into the air, Carol stuffed her hands into her jacket pocket and closed her eyes. She could handle this. She could go back to her regular life and live without Ben and the children, even if she had to take it one painful, lonely moment at a time.

As soon as the sleigh was cleared for landing and Carol stepped foot onto the North Pole she was swept into a flurry of activity that befit Christmas World Headquarters on the twenty-third of December.

"Welcome home, Carol," chorused dozens of Santa's helpers as she walked down the long gleaming corridor that led to Christmas Central. She waved and smiled as she continued on her way but she didn't stop to speak with anyone. Her heart was too heavy.

She stood outside her father's double oak office doors and took a moment to compose herself as best she could. Her father wouldn't be angry with her because she hadn't convinced Ben to love Christmas, she knew that. She'd never seen Santa angry. Knowing him, he wouldn't even be disappointed, which, some-how, made it all the harder to bear.

She took a deep breath and pushed open the door. Her heart felt a rush of warmth when she saw her father studying an old fashioned world map hung on the back wall of his office. She didn't have to speak because he turned at the sound of the door.

A loving smile stretched across his face and his blue eyes shone. "Carol, my lovely girl, welcome home." He held out his arms and she ran to him and hugged him more fiercely than she'd ever done before.

"Honey, honey, it's all going to work out." He held her at arm's length and searched her face. "I promise we'll sort through this."

She shook her head and wiped away the few tears that escaped her eyes. "No Dad, there's nothing to sort out. I'm sorry about-"

Santa held up a white gloved hand to stop her apology. "Hush, child. You've nothing to apologize for. In fact, your mother and I were just saying this morning that you did us proud with the way you handled everything at the Hanson's. You saved Christmas for those two children and that is a precious gift. Now, do you want to talk about your Ben now or later?"

"He's not my Ben, Dad." Carol put her hand over her chest in a futile effort to stop her heart from aching. "What I really want to do now is get to work."

"You've come to the right place then." Santa crossed to his desk, took a sheaf of papers from the top of a mountainous stack and handed them to her. "These are the conflicting naughty versus nice reports, and I need someone I can trust implicitly to make decisions."

Carol nodded. This she could do. "I'll just go and find Mom, say hello and then I'll get right to these."

"Thank you, my dear. Your mother is supervising the routine maintenance check on my sleigh, you know how she is about that."

"You two are lucky to have each other." She tried to smile but couldn't quite manage, not while she was fighting back tears.

"Luck has nothing to do with it. It's destiny."

"Not now, Dad, please." A change of subject was in order. Her younger sibling was always a safe distraction. "Where is Nicholas?"

Santa shook his head ruefully. "It seems as if both of my children have been busy falling in love. You with your Ben, and Nicholas with his new assistant. So, wherever the lovely Holly is, I wager so is your brother. Why you both couldn't have waited until January I can't fathom."

She was saved from a discussion she didn't want to have when the buzzer on Santa's desk sounded. She waited while he went to answer it.

Santa pushed the intercom button, "Claus One, here."

"We're looking for Claus Three," an elf responded.

Santa motioned Carol over to his desk. "Someone wants you."

Carol pressed the button, "Claus Three. Go ahead."

But she couldn't hear the response for the loud banging on the doors to Santa's office. "Hold, please," she said before letting go of the intercom. She waited while her father went to see what the commotion was all about.

Santa threw open the doors and an irate cadre of red faced elves charged into the office. Stunned at the angry energy they radiated, Carol went to stand beside her father.

"What's the meaning of this?" Santa asked, his voice calm yet authoritative.

Twenty angry voices chorused in a collectively irate response.

"One at a time," Santa demanded. "What's happened?"

Jolly pushed through the throng, dragging Rapz along with her. "Santa, we've got a situation."

"Situation my slippers," an elf in back shouted. "This is an emergency."

Carol glanced at her father. He was generally impervious to what others called emergencies. She tried to look Rapz in the eye but he wouldn't look up. That didn't bode well. "What's this all about, Jolly?"

The buzzer on the desk sounded again, it's low, shrill tone buzzing insistently. Carol ignored it.

"Tell them, Rapz, go ahead," Jolly ordered him. "I'm not doing your dirty work, start talking." She held up her hand for the crowd behind her to quiet down.

Rapz opened his mouth to speak but he was interrupted by the intercom.

"Oh, for holiday's sake." Santa strode around the desk and pushed the button. "Claus One here, requesting you cease harassing me with this blasted intercom."

"Sir, we need to speak with Claus Three. Immediately."

Santa's eyebrows rose. Immediately was usually an order he gave, not received. "Claus Three is busy. Out." He yanked on the chord until it came out of the socket. He smiled in satisfaction when the blinking light on the intercom went out.

"Now, Rapz, let's hear what you've done." Santa sank into his chair and motioned for the mob to move forward. They did, and Carol went to stand behind her father's chair.

"Sir, I was only trying to help."

"Rapz, today is December twenty-third. It's our last full day of pre-holiday operations so please just say what you have to say."

Rapz gulped. "I umm, well, I brought Carol a Christmas gift."

Carol and her father exchanged curious glances.

"Thank you, Rapz, but you know the rule," Carol said in a gentle voice. "The world needs their gifts delivered first before anyone here even thinks about opening their presents." She surveyed the seething group before turning her attention back to him. "Why is everyone so angry?"

"They don't like what I brought you."

This elicited deafening jeers that didn't stop until Santa thumped his desk with his fist. Several times. "Silence," he thundered.

Carol had never heard her father speak so sharply before, neither had any of the elves. Santa got his silence.

"Rapz, just answer my question. What gift did you get for my daughter?"

Rapz looked guiltily from Santa to Carol and then back at her father. "It's not so much a what, Sir, as a who."

"Who?" Santa repeated in confusion.

Before anyone else could speak, two small figures ran in through the open door and launched themselves at Carol.

"Hello, Miss Kane," they happily echoed each other.

Stunned, Carol looked down at Hillary and Patrick Hanson's upturned faces. The children were all but levitating with pure excitement but a ripple of dread ran through Carol. She stared at Rapz in disbelief and then tried to speak, but it took her more than one attempt to sound coherent. "You kidnapped Ben's children?"

CHAPTER 11

Carol's world swirled around her for a moment but any hope that this was all a bad joke vanished when Hillary tugged on her arm. She looked down. The children were really here, and in their pajamas no less.

"You woke them up?" she demanded of Rapz.

In answer, the elf stared intently at his upturned toes.

"No, he didn't, Miss Kane," Patrick said. "We couldn't sleep. The sleigh ride was awesome."

"You didn't tell us you knew Santa Claus," Hillary said, her gaze going back and forth between Carol and Santa as if she was trying to piece the whole picture together. "Do you know what the best part of this is? Daddy has to believe in Santa now." Hillary and her brother exchanged high fives.

"Ben is here?" Carol felt the world start to spin again. "He's here at the North Pole?"

"Of course I brought him along," Rapz snapped. "I might occasionally get my directions mixed up but I'm no kidnapper."

Mixed up? This went far, far beyond a mix up.

"Where is he?" she asked the elf. "I need to see him, to explain." Just how on earth she was going to do this she couldn't begin to imagine, but she had to see him and try to help him make sense of…well…being at the North Pole.

When Rapz wasn't forthcoming with an answer, Carol turned to Jolly. "Have you seen him? Do you know where he is?"

Jolly nodded. "He's in the infirmary but I think you should wait to see him until he regains consciousness."

Carol's eyes widened. She turned to her father, but his look of bewilderment was less than comforting.

"Now, children," Santa said to Hillary and Patrick, "I want you to go with these nice elves for a tour of my workshop." He motioned for Tinsel and Jolly to lead the way. "I'm sure there will be a few toys for you to test along the way."

They turned their bright, shining eyes to Carol for permission and she nodded. "Just stay close to Tinsel and Jolly. And don't worry about your Daddy, he'll be fine."

As soon as the children were out of ear shot she turned to Rapz. "Take me to Ben." Half way out the door she turned back to her father. "No, Daddy, you stay here. You have enough work to do. I need to take care of this myself."

After Rapz assured her that Ben wasn't seriously injured, she was able to calm down enough to listen to his version of events as they wound their way through the corridors to the infirmary. According to Rapz, he'd only meant to take the children for a quick ride but Ben had climbed up on the roof and freaked out when he saw his children in the sleigh.

"He reached for them but slipped, fell and hit his head."

"So you stuffed him in the sleigh and brought him here?" Carol asked.

Rapz shrugged. "I panicked."

Carol raised an eyebrow. "You understand that the unauthorized use of a sleigh is grounds for immediate demotion, don't you?"

Rapz nodded. "I know, I know. But the kids were really digging Christmas so I thought, hey, what could be better than giving them a spin around a few rooftops?"

"Rapz, children dig a lot of things. But that doesn't mean they get to try them all." Carol resisted the urge to box his pointed little ears. "I thought they were sound asleep with the forget-me dust."

"Well, that's just the thing. I came to pick you up but Jolly got there first. I didn't know that, see? So I went in the window to see what was taking you so long, I found the kids in the hallway."

They passed by the Naughty and Nice Records Department and Carol felt a pang of guilt that she'd not been able to help her father. "What was the silver sparkle supposed to do?"

"That was a bit of an experiment gone awry," Rapz conceded. "You see, I was thinking-"

But Carol had heard enough. "You weren't thinking, Rapz, and look what you've done." She stopped outside the infirmary door. "We can't have people here."

"I know. I'm sorry," Rapz said. "Do you want me to go in there and explain everything to your boyfriend?"

Carol shook her head. "No, you've already done enough. I think you'd better get right back to my father's office and do what you can to help him. We've only got a few hours before the countdown starts."

Once he was out of sight, Carol took a deep breath. Her heart was racing and, as much as she didn't want to admit it, there was a part of her that was thrilled that she was going to see Ben again. She held little hope, however, that the feeling was going to be mutual.

She gingerly opened the door and poked her head in the room. Her heart sank when she saw Ben's form on the infirmary table. She slipped through the open door and pulled it quietly closed behind her.

Wanda, an elderly female elf motioned for her to come closer. "Your friend here will be just fine, honey," she said as Carol approached.

Carol looked down at Ben, her heart swelling in her chest. Even though she knew she was in for it when he came to, she was happy to see him again. "Will he be okay?" she asked Wanda.

The nurse elf nodded. "He just bumped his head, he'll be fine. But I'm glad you're here because I had no idea what to say when he woke up and wanted to know where he was."

Greatly relieved, Carol sank into a chair next to Ben. She smiled her gratitude to Wanda. "Thank you so much for everything. But if it's just a matter of waiting for him to regain consciousness maybe it's better if I wait alone. It might make it easier when he wakes up and only sees me."

"Wise idea, dear," Wanda agreed. "I'll be in the business center typing up my incident report if you need me."

After the door closed behind her, Carol took one of Ben's hands and held it in hers. He looked like he was asleep. Knowing she shouldn't let her mind go there, she couldn't help but wonder what it would be like to wake up next to him every day for the rest of her life. It could only ever be a fantasy, and more likely than not, Ben would never want to see her again after she managed to get them safely home again. Still, despite the futility of it, she indulged in thoughts of a lifetime spent with Ben, Hillary and Patrick.

Four days ago she would have assured anyone who asked that she loved her life at the North Pole. And it would have been true then. But now she couldn't convince herself that she'd ever be happy again. Not without Ben, or his children.

Impulsively, knowing this would be the only chance

she'd ever have, she leaned over and brushed a kiss across Ben's lips.

BEN'S EYELIDS FLUTTERED OPEN. So it hadn't been a dream. Carol had kissed him. He smiled up at her, enjoying the surprised look on her face. Ah, so she'd thought she'd sneak in a quick kiss before leaving but he wouldn't let her go, not after last night. What had happened last night? He frowned trying to remember the details but his memory was foggy, almost as if he'd had too much to drink. No, that wasn't it. He'd fallen and hit his head. But where? How?

"Ben," Carol's voice cut through his reverie. "Can you hear me?"

He nodded and tried to sit up but he felt a restraining hand on his shoulder. Ah, so she wanted more. He reached for her and pulled her into a kiss, savoring the taste of her lips equally as much as her willingness to be kissed. When he released her, he could see by her expression that she was worried.

"Are you okay, Ben?"

"I could use another kiss," he teased her.

"Be serious, we were worried about you."

Reluctantly he dragged his attention from Carol and looked around. He wasn't at home. "Where am I?"

"There was a little accident," Carol said.

Panic coursed through him and he struggled to a

sitting position. "The kids, where are Patrick and Hillary? Are they hurt?"

"They're fine. They weren't hurt, only you were," Carol assured him, but by the way she was biting her lip he could tell there was much she was leaving unsaid.

He looked around, trying to get a sense of where he was. One glance told him he wasn't in the local hospital. This looked more like a school nurse's office. He frowned again and tried to read Carol's face. "Where am I?"

She shifted away from him, clearly uncomfortable. "This is going to take some explaining." She wrung her hands and watched him warily. "Can we just get you home first? If you'll just wait here I'll get us a...um... some transportation."

Transportation? Despite the dull ache in his head, he struggled to remember how he'd fallen. At home? No. Whatever had happened to him was just out of reach but at any minute it would come back. He just had to think backwards to the last thing he remembered. The party? No. Wait, he'd seen the kids climb into a sleigh, but where had they been that there was a sleigh?

"I can explain," Carol said. But she didn't. She just stared at him.

"Explain what?" he asked. Perhaps the kids had climbed up on a holiday display that they weren't supposed to and when he'd tried to get them out, he'd fallen. Yes, that must be it. He'd been upset with the kids because they'd climbed into a sleigh, and he'd seen Carol's friend from the mall just before he'd slipped.

He looked at Carol for confirmation, but before he could speak, the door opened and Patrick and Hillary ran in, a concerned looking Santa Claus close on their heels. Ben turned to Carol. "Are we at the mall?"

She groaned. "I wish."

CHAPTER 12

Carol watched as Ben embraced his children as best he could with one arm. The children were talking well over a mile a minute, and one glance at Ben told her that he was having trouble making sense of what they were saying. But she knew it was only a temporary reprieve.

"Okay, okay," Ben interrupted them, "let's go home and then you can tell me everything."

"Go home?" Patrick stepped back, alarm registering on his little features. "Why would we want to do that?"

"So that you can sleep," Ben answered his son's question. "I don't know what time the mall closes but it's getting late."

Hillary giggled. "The mall? Daddy, we're not at the mall!"

"We're not?" Ben glanced at Santa and then at her. "Okay, someone tell me what is going on here." When they didn't answer he pushed himself off the examining table and turned to her. "Carol? Where are we?"

She swallowed hard. There was nothing for it but to tell him the truth. "The North Pole."

"Oh, for the love of God, Carol, cut it out. This isn't funny anymore."

"It's true, Daddy. We're at the North Pole," Hillary said. She turned to point at Carol's father. "Just ask Santa. He'll tell you."

"Welcome to our home, Mr. Hanson," Santa said.

Carol cringed at Ben's incredulous expression. It was even worse to watch him gently guide the children toward the door as if he was escaping a lunatic asylum.

"Ben, wait, I can explain." Except, of course, that she couldn't.

"So you keep saying," he replied. He shot her a concerned glance. "I'm worried about you, Carol. I want you to come home with us. We can see someone about this Christmas obsession you have. I'll get you the help you need."

"Daddy, don't talk to Miss Kane like that," Hillary interjected. "She's not crazy."

Hillary's swift and heartfelt defense brought tears to Carol's eyes but she willed them away. If Ben saw her cry he'd be forever convinced she'd lost her mind.

"Well, I'm not going anywhere without my new puppy." Patrick pulled his hand free of his father's hold and ran to hug Carol.

"And I'm not leaving without Patrick." Hillary ran over and embraced Carol.

"Oh, now enough of that," Carol told them as sternly as she could manage. "We don't demand anything from Santa." Carol hugged them both to her, savoring the feel of their arms around her waist. Thinking of how much she was going to miss them made it hard to breathe. But she needed to get control of this situation. "Dad, it's getting late. I can handle this. You need to get down to command central."

"Dad?" Ben sounded incredulous. And, just as Carol expected, more than a bit freaked out.

Santa pulled out an old fashioned watch and checked the time before slipping it back in his pocket. He sighed. "I don't like leaving you."

"You don't have a choice, do you?" she gently reminded him. Time wasn't on his side and they both knew it. "Go, I can do this."

She waited while Santa bid farewell to the children and left before she spoke to them. Ben was way past believing her, but she could enlist his children's help. "Let's give your father a tour. I wonder if he's ever seen a reindeer before?"

"Carol, you're scaring me." Ben reached out and held her hand in his. "I can help you."

"Okay, you win," she said, changing tactics. "I'm ready to go home."

Ben's relieved smile made her feel guilty for setting him up. But she couldn't think of any other way to maneuver him into a sleigh other than pretending to leave with them.

"You know how to get to the parking lot?" he asked.

111

She nodded. "Just follow me, and umm, you're bound to see some holiday craziness on the way out."

"I can handle last minute shoppers," he assured her, his relief patently obvious. "Let's go, kids."

A perplexed looking Hillary and Patrick allowed themselves to be led from the room. Carol felt guilty for confusing them, but once she could get them sprinkled with green forget-me dust it wouldn't matter. The last twenty four hours would feel like a dream to them. This time she wouldn't trust Rapz though, she'd snag some of the good stuff on the way down to the departure area.

BEN FOLLOWED Carol and the children through the door and out into a corridor. She turned right and strode down the hall. His head throbbed and his shoulder smarted but it was nothing compared to the ache in his heart. He loved Carol. The moment she'd kissed him, he'd known that he would love her forever. But what could be wrong with her? Had a childhood trauma during the holidays scarred her for life?

Whatever it was, they'd get to the bottom of it. Together.

"Look out," Hillary called out. "A pile of presents is coming through."

Duly warned, Ben joined the others as they flattened themselves against the wall. An old-fashioned push cart piled seven feet high with brightly wrapped gift boxes sailed past them. The three elves pushing it all called out cheery greetings to Carol. How did they know her name?

The further along the apparently endless corridor that they went, the more bizarre the situation became. How many little people could possibly work in the same place? Ben knew he hadn't ever spent much time at the mall but it couldn't be this large. The hallway widened with each step they took until it became downright cavernous.

"Hey, Carol," a man with dark hair, about Ben's own age, approached them, a huge smile on his face. "Oh, have I missed you. I knew you'd make it back in time."

The stranger threw his arms around Carol and, to Ben's annoyance, she willingly accepted his embrace. Who the heck was this?

Carol pulled back, rather reluctantly Ben thought, and linked her arm through the man's. "Nick, I'd like you to meet my friends. This is Hillary Hanson and her brother Patrick. And this is…this is Ben."

"Ah, Ben, nice to finally meet you," Nick said. He reached out shake Ben's hand and then the children's. "I've heard a great deal about you three."

"Funny, Carol never mentioned you once," Ben replied.

"Never mentioned her charming, intelligent brother?" Nick shook his head in mock bewilderment, which caused the children to laugh.

"Is your last name Kane too?" Patrick asked.

It wasn't lost on Ben that Nick and Carol exchanged a quick conspiratorial glance.

"You can call me St. Nick," Nick said, earning grins from the children.

Ben managed not to roll his eyes, but just barely. St. Nick? And his poor Carol, she thought the bearded retiree was her father and this joker was her brother? Not likely. Not unless they were all members of some sort of Christmas themed circus.

Like a light bulb switching on in a dark broom closet, Ben's mind suddenly flooded with understanding. He got it. He knew what was going on, he knew where they were. And he knew what Carol was involved in. This whole set up reminded him of a back-stage tour of an ice capades show he'd been on when he was around eight years old. The flurry of activity, the costumes, the props, and Santa and the elves staying in character, it was all a part of some traveling Christmas show.

But why hadn't Carol just said so? There was no shame in theater. Sure it was a little odd but weren't most creative types at least a tiny bit eccentric? His heart warmed knowing that the woman he loved wasn't crazy.

"So, when's show time?" he interrupted Carol and Nick's conversation.

They both turned to stare at him.

"I get it, I know where we are." He smiled just a bit triumphantly. "Live theater, and done on an impressive scale I have to say. I'd love to know what the budget for something like this runs."

"The holidays are priceless," Nick said. "None of this is about money."

"Yeah, right, Christmas isn't about money," Ben scoffed.

"Not now, Daddy," Hillary said.

He glanced down, feeling suddenly guilty. He knew he should let the children have their fun. "Sorry," he managed to say. "Carol, why don't you help us find our seats? That way you can get in costume and we'll all go home together after the performance."

Carol stood looking at him without saying a word. Until Nick nudged her.

"That's right, Carol, help them find their seats. Unless you'd like me to take them for you? I'd be happy to if it's easier for you."

"No thank you, Nick. It's something I need to do."

Why did she look so stricken? Ben wanted to reach out to her, to pull her close and reassure her but this wasn't the place or the time. They'd have to wait until after the show was over and they were home, but what could that be, a matter of a few hours?

"Nice to meet you all," Nick said, and with a quick kiss for Carol and a wave to the children, he was swept up in to yet another wave of gift carrying elves all heading down the hallway.

Carol didn't meet Ben's eye or say a word as they wound through the seemingly never-ending corridor. Ben marveled at the sheer size of the cast as well as the size of the set. Once he got home he wanted to google this production company to see what he could learn, there had to be some serious clout behind a show this size. Obviously no expense had been spared. Even the air smelled like evergreens. Amazing.

They stopped outside a wooden door with a brass plate that read 'Christmas Magic'. He did as she asked and waited while Carol slipped through the door to what he assumed was the box office.

"This is going to be some kind of show," he said to his children.

"Daddy, what are you talking about?" Hillary demanded. "We're at the North Pole."

"Are we?" He might as well play along. "What do you think Patrick?"

His son didn't miss a beat. "We've ridden in a sleigh, we've seen Santa, met the elves and got to see Santa's workshop. Yeah, we're so at the North Pole."

With a sad smile, Carol rejoined them. "Thanks for waiting, we're almost there." She took ahold of both children's hands and continued on the way. Ben followed, thinking that all the craziness aside, it felt so right to see Carol with his children. He knew she'd love them as her own. A new mother and a happy family, this was the perfect Christmas present for his children. For him too.

True to her word they arrived in front of a door marked 'Departures' a few moments later. He followed as Carol pushed the double doors open. The smell of livestock assailed his senses, immediately followed by a blast of air colder than he'd ever felt.

"Let's get you into your jackets," Carol said as she took them off the rack and handed them out.

Ben took his from her. "Thank you," and then wishing he could bring a smile to her face, he teased her, "We must be VIP's to have our jackets ready and waiting."

"Daddy, what's a VIP?" Patrick asked.

Carol, her eyes moist with tears, bent down to kiss Patrick's cheek. "Very important person." She gave Hillary a kiss as well and then hugged them both. "And you will always be very important to me." She straightened and wiped away a tear from the corner of her eye before letting out a low whistle.

Within seconds a sleigh with eight animals harnessed to it pulled up in front of them. His children clapped and danced in place. He didn't share their excitement. He stared at the animals and at the wizened elf actor who sat in the driver's seat. "What are these animals, Carol? Caribou?"

"Reindeer, Daddy, aren't you silly that you don't know that. Come on." Patrick ran to the sleigh and climbed in. His sister was only a step behind them.

"They're safe, Ben."

He wasn't so sure. "Just sit down and don't move. I'll be right there." The sight of his children in the sleigh triggered his memory, at least partially. "They took a ride already, didn't they? This is where I fell?"

"Yes, they took a ride but you didn't fall here. You

were…never mind. It doesn't matter anymore." She wiped away another tear.

Watching her cry hurt his heart. He reached out to pull her close and hold her in his arms. It felt so right. He kissed the top of her head and, when she looked up, he leaned his forehead against hers for a long moment. "I love you."

Her next words were not what he hoped to hear. "You'd better go. It's time." She pulled away from him and smiled through her tears.

"I don't want to go." He didn't. Despite the fact he didn't know exactly where he was, he wanted to be with her. "Let's go home. There has to be some understudy who can play your part. You should be with us tonight."

She shook her head. "I want to be with you but I need to be here." She waved her hand in the direction of the sleigh. "Please, Ben, it's time for you to go."

Reluctantly he climbed in and pulled Patrick onto his lap. "We'll see you right after the show." He started to tell her to break a leg but stopped when she pulled a silver velvet pouch from her pocket and opened it. Why was she reaching into it? "Wait, Carol, what is that?"

She took a handful of green glitter and tossed it toward them. He watched as it swirled up and around the sleigh before it fell like snowflakes all over them.

Just as the sleigh started to pull away, he heard her softly answer his question. "It's all a part of the show."

CHAPTER 13

"I like traveling by sleigh better than this stinky old airplane."

"Eat your peanuts, Patrick." Ben leaned back against the head rest and closed his eyes. They were three hours out from LAX and still hours away from landing in Maui. That wasn't even counting the several hours they'd spent in flight just to reach Los Angeles. On top of that, Christmas Eve had been a sad state of affairs at their home, Christmas Day itself had been even worse. The person who first said that misery loved company had really known what they were talking about.

"Another thing I liked better about traveling by sleigh is the fresh air," Patrick groused. "This plane is stuffy and the window won't open."

Ben counted to ten. Twice. He turned to his daughter, who sat in the middle seat. "Hillary, can you please play another game of tic tac toe with your brother?"

"I'd like to Daddy, but I'm too worried about the new puppy that we left at home," Hillary said. "You remember the one, the stuffed puppy that isn't real? The one that doesn't play, the one I have to pretend to take care of?" She stared straight ahead, as if the back of the seat in front of her fascinated her. Her arms folded over her chest was an obvious signal that she had exactly zero interest in continuing their conversation.

"Hillary, you know that stuffed dog was a place holder until we get the chance to get a real dog."

She spared him a sideways glance. "If you really believed in Santa Claus then he would have brought us a real dog."

"I do believe in Santa Claus." He did. He was crazy. Insane. Certifiable was the only word for it. He did believe in Santa, he did believe the North Pole existed, hell, he'd actually been there. But once the sleigh had dropped them off at home he'd had no idea how to reach Carol to tell her so.

He'd been heartbroken until he'd heard from his kids that Carol's family vacationed in Maui every year right after Christmas. Then he'd taken time off of work, thrown a handful of summer clothes in a suit-case, and spent a fortune on last minute plane tickets. All on the slim hope that he could find Carol and convince her that he could make her happy.

Ben shifted in his seat and stuck his leg out into the aisle in a futile effort to get comfortable. He was miser-able, but it wasn't jet lag that was responsible for his misery. He missed Carol. He loved her. And he could only pray she felt the same way. A niggling voice in his head demanded to know why she'd sent them away from the North Pole if she cared about them? He could only hope it was because she didn't think he believed. But he did believe. In Santa, in the North Pole, in the whole nine yards. Love did crazy things to a man's mind. That much he would never doubt again.

He patted the jewelers box in his chest pocket again for reassurance. Hillary and Patrick thought they remembered the name of Santa's condo development. That was all he had to go on once they landed. It wasn't much information but it was a start. If need be, he'd comb the island until they found the Claus family because there wasn't a chance he was ringing in the New Year without the woman he loved.

CAROL PULLED a yellow sun dress from the closet, wadded it into a ball and shoved it into her suitcase. She threw in a pair of sandals and topped it off with her swimsuit before zipping it up and dropping it by the door.

"Are you sure you have to go, sweetheart?"

"Oh, Mom, I don't know." Carol sank onto the bed and buried her face in her hands.

"Honey, don't cry." Her mother sat next to her and pulled Carol into a comforting hug. "Have a little faith."

Carol pulled back and wiped the tears from her

face. "How? Ben doesn't believe in Santa, the North Pole, or Christmas. Not any of it." She took a deep shuddering breath. "So there is no way we can make this work."

"No way?"

Carol shook her head. "None. It would never work. We come from two different worlds and there is no middle ground."

"You're right." Mrs. Claus stood and smoothed out the wrinkles on the bedspread. "Maybe it's for the best. Granted, I haven't yet met this young man but if he doesn't have a big enough heart to-"

"Mother!" Carol frowned. "Ben is a kind and loving man."

"I'm sure he is dear," Mrs. Claus replied, her voice steady and matter of fact. "But the fact remains that he is a father to two young children and, from what you've told me, he did everything he could to ruin their Christmas."

"That's not fair," Carol protested. "Ben is a wonderful father. He loves Hillary and Patrick. And he didn't try to ruin their Christmas. Just the opposite actually, he was trying to protect them from being hurt or disappointed any more than they already have been."

"So why did he struggle to believe that you were your father's daughter? If he really cared about you then why didn't he just instantly accept the whole situation?"

Carol fought against a rush of frustration and anger. "I am shocked you are being so cold hearted,

Mother. Do you have any idea how much of a stretch it would be for any man to just automatically believe that Santa was real, that the North Pole existed, and that reindeer really fly? You are judging Ben way too harshly."

"Yes, you are."

Carol opened her mouth but quickly closed it. "What did you just say?"

Her mother smiled. "I agree with everything you just said. You're right, it is unfair to blame the poor man because he needed time to adjust to the fact that not only is Santa real, but that he'd fallen in love with Santa's daughter."

Carol stared at her mother for a long moment before a slow smile spread across her face. "Oh, you're good, Mom."

"Thank you. I've had years of practice on your father." She winked. "I only wanted to point out that Ben isn't the only man who is slow to come around. Men aren't encouraged to believe in things like Santa Claus and Christmas magic. Before they're even teenagers, young men are expected to become prag-matic and tough minded. So, can't you understand that he'd need time to process all of this?"

Her mother's words gave Carol's heart hope. It made so much sense. She'd been so rigid in her way of thinking that she hadn't seen Ben's side of things. But as quickly as her hopes rose, they were dashed again by another thought.

"But, Mom, I sprinkled forget-me dust on Ben and

the children when they left the North Pole. I really poured it on thick too." Carol felt her eyes fill with tears. "Ben and the kids won't remember me."

"I wouldn't be so sure of that."

She eyed her mother, afraid to hope. "What do you mean?"

Mrs. Claus smiled. "Forget-me dust is magical and wonderful but it has a little drawback."

"Drawback?"

"It doesn't work on loved ones. And that means...," Mrs. Claus let her voice trail off.

"That Ben hasn't forgotten me." Carol felt as if this loop hole was the most precious gift she'd ever received. "I mean, if he cares about me that is. So if I go to see him, and if he recognizes me, that means he loves me."

Carol's mother hugged her close. "That's exactly right. So, now what are you going to do?"

"I'm going back to the mainland."

"Let's go see your father about booking a flight." Carol's mother opened the door and ushered her daughter out. "It would be so much easier to send for a sleigh, wouldn't it?"

Carol shook her head. "Dad would never go for it. He'd call it reindeer abuse if we asked any time before February."

THE TAXI SWUNG into the Mele Kalikimaka Cove

Condominium driveway and stopped in front of the main double doors. The driver alighted, took the bags from the trunk and opened the cab door. Hillary and Patrick jumped out, Ben only a step behind them. He handed the driver two twenties and couldn't resist asking once more if this was the only development on Maui with the word Christmas in its name.

"Yes, sir," the driver said, slipping the fare into the chest pocket of his brightly patterned Hawaiian shirt. "I've lived here all my life and don't know of any other place that fits the bill. Mele Kalikimaka is Hawaiian for Merry Christmas so this loosely translates to Merry Christmas Cove." His expression was puzzled. "You want me to wait for you just in case you've got the wrong place?"

"No, thank you," Ben said. "This has to be it." He glanced down at Hillary and Patrick's tired but suddenly eager faces. If he couldn't find Carol it would break their little hearts as much as his. Nothing like a little pressure.

"We're in the right place, Daddy." Hillary said, her voice sounding much more assured than he felt. "Just look at the building."

Ben looked up. He'd never seen a set of condos that were so pristinely white. The windows were all arch shaped. The awning over the front door was red and all of the wooden flower planters were painted a bright green. "I think you might be right, Hillary."

"What do we do now?" Patrick asked. "Knock on every door?"

Ben shook his head. That would take too long. He surveyed the building again. It looked as if almost all the units had their windows open to take advantage of the blissful island breeze.

The idea that he could be only minutes away from seeing Carol again helped him shed his last inhibition. He lifted one hand and cupped it around his mouth, all the better for his voice to carry. "Santa," he yelled. "Santa Claus. I know you're here. I need to see you."

A few curtains wavered but he couldn't tell if the breeze was moving them or if curious condo owners were peeking out to see who the shouting lunatic was. He waited until a middle aged couple in swim suits walked by before trying again. "Santa, send down your daughter." He paused for only a moment. "I love her."

"CAROL, you'd better hurry down there before that young man of yours blows my cover." Santa slipped his arm around his wife's shoulder, their delighted smiles indicating their approval. "And for the love of Christmas, say yes to whatever he asks so we can get some quiet."

With a grateful grin, Carol headed out the door and ran down the stairway as quickly as she could. It felt like her heart gave her feet wings. Ben was here. He remembered her. He loved her!

She pushed open the lobby door and looked

around. Joy filled her heart when she saw three suitcases, two children, and the one man she'd love forever.

Their eyes met and for one perfect moment the rest of the world ceased to exist. Carol wasn't sure if she went to Ben, or if he came to her, but suddenly he was holding her close and that was all she cared about.

"You came." She pulled back to smile up at him.

"We did," Ben said, standing back just far enough to allow Hillary and Patrick to hug her. "We have something to ask you."

Carol's eyes great moist with tears of joy. "You've come all this way," she said. "So ask me."

She watched as Ben nodded to the children and then all three spoke in unison, "Will you marry us?"

Carol nodded, momentarily unable to speak. Tears of happiness slipped down her cheeks. She bent and hugged the children tightly, loving the feeling of their arms around her neck, their little faces pressed to hers. "Yes, I will." She glanced up at Ben and saw her own joy reflected in his eyes. "Now, do you two want to run upstairs and tell my parents the good news?" At their eager nods she said, "They're in Unit 200. Up the stairs and the first door on the right."

As soon as she saw they were safely in the building she turned back to Ben. Her fiancé. The wonder of it filled her heart.

"Marry me?" he asked, his voice was thick with emotion. He pulled a black velvet box out of his pocket and opened it. "Please?"

Carol gasped. Nestled in the velvet was a gold band

with a brilliant diamond flanked by an emerald on one side and a ruby on the other. "It's beautiful," she finally managed to say. "They're Christmas colors."

He nodded and slipped the ring out of the box and onto her finger. It was a perfect fit. She held her hand up and marveled at how perfect her world suddenly had become. She looked up at him. "Ben, but what about, you know, the whole holiday and my family thing?"

He smiled. "I'm fine with it, Carol. We'll work it out. I mean, everyone has in-laws to get used to, right?"

She laughed.

He leaned down and kissed her. When at last she pulled back, he took her hands in his and held them up against his chest, over his heart. "I believe, Carol. In Christmas, in your father, in magic, in it all."

"What happened?" She slipped her arms around his neck and looked up at him. "What made you change your mind?"

He cocked his head, pretending to think. "It could have been a couple of things. One, I met the most incredible woman in the world who stole my heart, or it could have been flying over rooftops in a sleigh pulled by reindeer. I think we can safely say that either would make a believer out of any man."

"I love you," she said.

"I love you too. Now, I'd like to go meet your mother and thank your father."

"Thank him? For what?"

Ben grinned. "For so many things." He kissed her

again. "For giving me hope, for giving the kids and I happiness, for raising such an incredible daughter."

Carol smiled. "You believe."

He nodded, a playful smile on his lips. "I love the holidays. In fact, I'm already counting down the days until next Christmas."

She laughed. "You are going to make a great Claus."

Note from Caroline:

Thank you for reading *Miss Kane's Christmas.* I hope you enjoyed your time at the North Pole! Please visit my author website to learn more about my other holiday novellas set at Christmas Central. If you enjoy reading holiday-themed romances as much as I do, I invite you to visit my website, The Christmas Bookshelf, which is devoted to Christmas romance novels. I appreciate the time you spent reading this story and I would be especially grateful if you would consider leaving a review where you originally purchased this e-book. Thank you!

www.carolinemickelson.com
www.thechristmasbookshelf.com

Printed in Great Britain
by Amazon